THE MIRROR
OF THE SEA

THE MIRROR OF THE SEA

Joseph Conrad

WILDSIDE PRESS

Doylestown, Pennsylvania

The Mirror of the Sea
A publication of
WILDSIDE PRESS
P.O. Box 301
Holicong, PA 18928-0301

www.wildsidepress.com

Chapter I

"And shippes by the brinke comen and gon,
And in swich forme endure a day or two."
The Frankeleyn's Tale

*L*andfall and Departure mark the rhythmical swing of a seaman's life and of a ship's career. From land to land is the most concise definition of a ship's earthly fate.

A "Departure" is not what a vain people of landsmen may think. The term "Landfall" is more easily understood; you fall in with the land, and it is a matter of a quick eye and of a clear atmosphere. The Departure is not the ship's going away from her port anymore than the Landfall can be looked upon as the synonym of arrival. But there is this difference in the Departure: that the term does not imply so much a sea event as a definite act entailing a process — the precise observation of certain landmarks by means of the compass card.

Your Landfall, be it a peculiarly-shaped mountain, a rocky headland, or a stretch of sand-dunes, you meet at first with a single glance. Further recognition will follow in due course; but essentially a Landfall, good or bad, is made and done with at the first cry of "Land ho!" The Departure is distinctly a ceremony of navigation. A ship may have left her port some time before; she may have been at sea, in the fullest sense of the phrase, for days; but, for all that, as long as the coast she was about to leave remained in sight, a southern-going ship of yesterday had not in the sailor's sense begun the enterprise of a passage.

The taking of Departure, if not the last sight of the land, is, perhaps, the last professional recognition of the land on the part of a sailor. It is the technical, as distinguished from the sentimental, "good-bye." Henceforth he has done with the coast astern of his ship. It is a matter personal to the man. It is not the ship that takes her departure; the seaman takes his Departure by means of cross-bearings which fix the place of the first tiny pencil-cross on the white expanse of the track-chart, where the ship's position at noon shall be marked by just such another tiny pencil cross for every day of her passage. And there may be sixty, eighty, any number of these crosses on the ship's track from land to land. The greatest number in my experience was a hundred and thirty of such crosses from the pilot station at the Sand Heads in the Bay of Bengal to the Scilly's light. A bad passage . . .

A Departure, the last professional sight of land, is always good, or at least good enough. For, even if the weather be thick, it does not matter much to a ship having all the open sea before her bows. A Landfall may be good or bad. You encompass the earth with one particular spot of it in your eye. In all the devious tracings the course of a sailing-ship leaves upon the white paper of a chart she is always aiming for that one little spot — maybe a small island in the ocean, a single headland upon the long coast of a continent, a lighthouse on a bluff, or simply the peaked form of a mountain like an ant-heap afloat upon the waters. But if you have sighted it on the expected bearing, then that Landfall is good. Fogs, snowstorms, gales thick with clouds and rain — those are the enemies of good Landfalls.

Chapter II

Some commanders of ships take their Departure from the home coast sadly, in a spirit of grief and discontent. They have a wife, children perhaps, some affection at any rate, or perhaps only some pet vice, that must be left behind for a year or more. I remember only one man who walked his deck with a springy step, and gave the first course of the passage in an elated voice. But he, as I learned afterwards, was leaving nothing behind him, except a welter of debts and threats of legal proceedings.

On the other hand, I have known many captains who, directly their ship had left the narrow waters of the Channel, would disappear from the sight of their ship's company altogether for some three days or more. They would take a long dive, as it were, into their state-room, only to emerge a few days afterwards with a more or less serene brow. Those were the men easy to get on with. Besides, such a complete retirement seemed to imply a satisfactory amount of trust in their officers, and to be trusted displeases no seaman worthy of the name.

On my first voyage as chief mate with good Captain

MacW——— I remember that I felt quite flattered, and went blithely about my duties, myself a commander for all practical purposes. Still, whatever the greatness of my illusion, the fact remained that the real commander was there, backing up my self-confidence, though invisible to my eyes behind a maple-wood veneered cabin door with a white china handle.

That is the time, after your Departure is taken, when the spirit of your commander communes with you in a muffled voice, as if from the sanctum sanctorum of a temple; because, call her a temple or a "hell afloat" — as some ships have been called — the captain's state-room is surely the august place in every vessel.

The good MacW——— would not even come out to his meals, and fed solitarily in his holy of holies from a tray covered with a white napkin. Our steward used to bend an ironic glance at the perfectly empty plates he was bringing out from there. This grief for his home, which overcomes so many married seamen, did not deprive Captain MacW——— of his legitimate appetite. In fact, the steward would almost invariably come up to me, sitting in the captain's chair at the head of the table, to say in a grave murmur, "The captain asks for one more slice of meat and two potatoes." We, his officers, could hear him moving about in his berth, or lightly snoring, or fetching deep sighs, or splashing and blowing in his bathroom; and we made our reports to him through the keyhole, as it were. It was the crowning achievement of his amiable character that the answers we got were given in a quite mild and friendly tone. Some commanders in their periods of seclusion are constantly grumpy, and seem to resent the mere sound of your voice as an injury and an insult.

But a grumpy recluse cannot worry his subordinates: whereas the man in whom the sense of duty is strong (or, perhaps, only the sense of self-importance), and who persists in airing on deck his moroseness all day — and perhaps half the night — becomes a grievous infliction. He walks the poop darting gloomy glances, as though he wished to poison the sea, and snaps your head off savagely whenever you happen to blunder within earshot. And these vagaries are the harder to bear patiently, as becomes a man and an officer, because no sailor is really good-tempered during the first few days of a voyage. There are regrets, memories, the instinctive longing for the departed idleness, the instinctive hate of all work. Besides, things have a knack of going wrong at the start, especially in the matter of irritating trifles. And there is the abiding thought of a whole year of more or less hard life before one, because there was hardly a southern-going voyage in the yesterday of the sea which meant anything less than a twelvemonth. Yes; it needed a few days after the taking of your departure for a ship's company to shake down into their places, and for the soothing deep-water ship routine to establish its beneficent sway.

It is a great doctor for sore hearts and sore heads, too, your ship's routine, which I have seen soothe — at least for a time — the most turbulent of spirits. There is health in it, and peace, and satisfaction of the accomplished round; for each day of the ship's life seems to close a circle within the wide ring of the sea horizon. It borrows a certain dignity of sameness from the majestic monotony of the sea. He who loves the sea loves also the ship's routine.

Nowhere else than upon the sea do the days, weeks and months fall away quicker into the past. They seem to be left astern as easily as the light air-bubbles in the swirls of the ship's wake, and vanish into a great silence in which your ship moves on with a sort of magical effect. They pass away, the days, the weeks, the months. Nothing but a gale can disturb the orderly life of the ship; and the spell of unshaken monotony that seems to have fallen upon the very voices of her men is broken only by the near prospect of a Landfall.

Then is the spirit of the ship's commander stirred strongly again. But it is not moved to seek seclusion, and to remain, hidden and inert, shut up in a small cabin with the solace of a good bodily appetite. When about to make the land, the spirit of the ship's commander is tormented by an unconquerable restlessness. It seems unable to abide for many seconds together in the holy of holies of the captain's state-room; it will out on deck and gaze ahead, through straining eyes, as the appointed moment comes nearer. It is kept vigorously upon the stretch of excessive vigilance. Meantime the body of the ship's commander is being enfeebled by want of appetite; at least, such is my experience, though "enfeebled" is perhaps not exactly the word. I might say, rather, that it is spiritualized by a disregard for food, sleep, and all the ordinary comforts, such as they are, of sea life. In one or two cases I have known that detachment from the grosser needs of existence remain regrettably incomplete in the matter of drink.

But these two cases were, properly speaking, pathological cases, and the only two in all my sea experience. In one of these two instances of a craving for stimulants, developed from sheer anxiety, I cannot assert that the man's seamanlike qualities were impaired in the least. It was a very anxious case, too, the land being made suddenly, close-to, on a wrong bearing, in thick weather, and during a fresh onshore gale. Going below to speak to him soon after, I was unlucky enough to catch my captain in the very act of hasty cork-drawing. The sight, I may say, gave me an awful scare. I was well aware of the morbidly sensitive nature of the man. Fortunately, I managed to draw back unseen, and, taking care to stamp heavily with my sea-boots at the foot of the cabin stairs, I made my second entry. But for this unexpected glimpse, no act of his during the next twenty-four hours could have given me the slightest suspicion that all was not well with his nerve.

Chapter III

Quite another case, and having nothing to do with drink, was that of poor Captain B——. He used to suffer from sick headaches, in his young days, every time he was approaching a coast. Well over fifty years of age when I knew him, short, stout, dignified, perhaps a little pompous, he was a man of a singularly well-informed mind, the least sailorlike in outward aspect, but certainly one of the best seamen whom it has been my good luck to serve under. He was a Plymouth man, I think, the son of a country doctor, and both his elder boys were studying medicine. He commanded a big London ship, fairly well known in her day. I thought no end of him, and that is why I remember with a peculiar satisfaction the last words he spoke to me on board his ship after an eighteen months' voyage. It was in the dock in Dundee, where we had brought a full cargo of jute from Calcutta. We had been paid off that morning, and I had come on board to take my sea-chest away and to say good-bye. In his slightly lofty but courteous way he inquired what were my plans. I replied that I intended leaving for London by the afternoon train, and thought of going up for examination to get my master's certificate. I had just enough service for that. He commended me for not wasting my time, with such an evident interest in my case that I was quite surprised; then, rising from his chair, he said:

"Have you a ship in view after you have passed?"

I answered that I had nothing whatever in view.

He shook hands with me, and pronounced the memorable words:

"If you happen to be in want of employment, remember that as long as I have a ship you have a ship, too."

In the way of compliment there is nothing to beat this from a ship's captain to his second mate at the end of a voyage, when the work is over and the subordinate is done with. And there is a pathos in that memory, for the poor fellow never went to sea again after all. He was already ailing when we passed St. Helena; was laid up for a time when we were off the Western Islands, but got out of bed to make his Landfall. He managed to keep up on deck as far as the Downs, where, giving his orders in an exhausted voice, he anchored for a few hours to send a wire to his wife and take aboard a North Sea pilot to help him sail the ship up the east coast. He had not felt equal to the task by himself, for it is the sort of thing that keeps a deep-water man on his feet pretty well night and day.

When we arrived in Dundee, Mrs. B——— was already there, waiting to take him home. We traveled up to London by the same train; but by the time I had managed to get through with my examination the ship had sailed on her next voyage without him, and, instead of joining her again, I went by request to see my old commander in his home. This is the only one of my captains I have ever visited in that way. He was out of bed by then, "quite convalescent," as he declared, making a few tottering steps to meet me at the sitting room door. Evidently he was reluctant to take his final cross-bearings of this earth for a Departure on the only voyage to an unknown destination a sailor ever undertakes. And it was all very nice — the large, sunny room; his deep, easy chair in a bow window, with pillows and a footstool; the quiet, watchful care of the elderly, gentle woman who had borne him five children, and had not, perhaps, lived with him more than five full years out of the thirty or so of their married life. There was also another woman there in a plain black dress, quite gray-haired, sitting very erect on her chair with some sewing, from which she snatched side-glances in his direction, and uttering not a single word during all the time of my call. Even when, in due course, I carried over to her a cup of tea, she only nodded at me silently, with the faintest ghost of a smile on her tight-set lips. I imagine she must have been a maiden sister of Mrs. B—— come to help nurse her brother-in-law. His youngest boy, a late-comer, a great cricketer it seemed, twelve years old or thereabouts, chattered enthusiastically of the exploits of W. G. Grace. And I remember his eldest son, too, a newly-fledged doctor, who took me out to smoke in the garden, and, shaking his head with professional gravity, but with genuine concern, muttered: "Yes, but he doesn't get back his appetite. I don't like that — I don't like that at all." The last sight of Captain B—— I had was as he nodded his head to me out of the bow window when I turned round to close the front gate.

It was a distinct and complete impression, something that I don't know whether to call a Landfall or a Departure. Certainly he had gazed at times very fixedly before him with the Landfall's vigilant look, this sea-captain seated incongruously in a deep-backed chair. He had not then talked to me of employment, of ships, of being ready to take another command; but he had discoursed of his early days, in the abundant but thin flow of a willful invalid's talk. The women looked worried, but sat still, and I learned more of him in that interview than in the whole eighteen months we had sailed together. It appeared he had "served his time" in the copper-ore trade, the famous copper-ore trade of old days between Swansea and the Chilean coast, coal out and ore in, deep-loaded both ways, as if in wanton defiance of the great Cape Horn seas — a work, this, for staunch ships, and a great school of staunchness for West-Country seamen. A whole fleet of copper-bottomed barques, as strong in rib and planking, as well-found in gear, as ever was sent upon the seas, manned by hardy crews and commanded by young masters, was engaged in that now long defunct trade. "That was the school I was trained in," he said to me almost boastfully, lying back amongst his pillows with a rug over his legs. And it was in that trade that he obtained his first command at a very early age. It was then that he mentioned to me how, as a young commander, he was always ill for a few days before making land after a long passage. But this sort of sickness used to pass off with the first sight of a familiar landmark. Afterwards, he added, as he grew older, all that nervousness wore off completely; and I observed his weary eyes gaze steadily ahead, as if there had been nothing between him and the straight line of sea and sky, where whatever a seaman is looking for is first bound to appear. But I have also seen his eyes rest fondly upon the faces in the room, upon the pictures on the wall, upon all the familiar objects of that home, whose abiding and clear image must have flashed often on his memory in times of stress and anxiety at sea. Was he looking out for a strange Landfall, or taking with an untroubled mind the bearings for his last

Departure?

It is hard to say; for in that voyage from which no man returns Landfall and Departure are instantaneous, merging together into one moment of supreme and final attention. Certainly I do not remember observing any sign of faltering in the set expression of his wasted face, no hint of the nervous anxiety of a young commander about to make land on an uncharted shore. He had had too much experience of Departures and Landfalls! And had he not "served his time" in the famous copper-ore trade out of the Bristol Channel, the work of the staunchest ships afloat, and the school of staunch seamen?

Chapter IV

*B*efore an anchor can ever be raised, it must be let go; and this perfectly obvious truism brings me at once to the subject of the degradation of the sea language in the daily press of this country.

Your journalist, whether he takes charge of a ship or a fleet, almost invariably "casts" his anchor. Now, an anchor is never cast, and to take a liberty with technical language is a crime against the clearness, precision, and beauty of perfected speech.

An anchor is a forged piece of iron, admirably adapted to its end, and technical language is an instrument wrought into perfection by ages of experience, a flawless thing for its purpose. An anchor of yesterday (because nowadays there are contrivances like mushrooms and things like claws, of no particular expression or shape — just hooks) — an anchor of yesterday is in its way a most efficient instrument. To its perfection its size bears witness, for there is no other appliance so small for the great work it has to do. Look at the anchors hanging from the cat-heads of a big ship! How tiny they are in proportion to the great size of the hull! Were they made of gold they would look like trinkets, like ornamental toys, no bigger in proportion than a jeweled drop in a woman's ear. And yet upon them will depend, more than once, the very life of the ship.

An anchor is forged and fashioned for faithfulness; give it ground that it can bite, and it will hold till the cable parts, and then, whatever may afterwards befall its ship, that anchor is "lost." The honest, rough piece of iron, so simple in appearance, has more parts than the human body has limbs: the ring, the stock, the crown, the flukes, the palms, the shank. All this, according to the journalist, is "cast" when a ship arriving at an anchorage is brought up.

This insistence in using the odious word arises from the fact that a particularly benighted landsman must imagine the act of anchoring as a process of throwing something overboard, whereas the anchor ready for its work is already overboard, and is not thrown over, but simply allowed to fall. It hangs from the ship's side at the end of a heavy, projecting timber called the cat-head, in the bight of a short, thick chain whose end link is suddenly released by a blow from a top-maul or the pull of a lever when the order is given. And the order is not "Heave over!" as the paragraphist seems to imagine, but "Let go!"

As a matter of fact, nothing is ever cast in that sense on board ship but the lead, of which a cast is taken to search the depth of water on which she floats. A lashed boat, a spare spar, a cask or what not secured about the decks, is "cast adrift" when it is untied. Also the ship herself is "cast to port or starboard" when getting under way. She, however, never "casts" her anchor.

To speak with severe technicality, a ship or a fleet is "brought up" — the complementary words unpronounced and unwritten being, of course, "to an anchor." Less technically, but not less correctly, the word "anchored," with its characteristic appearance and resolute sound, ought to be good enough for the newspapers of the greatest maritime country in the world. "The fleet anchored at Spithead": can anyone want a better sentence for brevity and seamanlike ring? But the "cast-anchor" trick, with its affectation of being a sea-phrase — for why not write just as well "threw anchor," "flung anchor," or 'shied anchor"? — is intolerably odious to a sailor's ear. I remember a coasting pilot of my early acquaintance (he used to read the papers assiduously) who, to define the utmost degree of lubberliness in a landsman, used to say, "He's one of them poor, miserable 'cast-anchor' devils."

Chapter V

*F*rom first to last the seaman's thoughts are very much concerned with his anchors. It is not so much that the anchor is a symbol of hope as that it is the heaviest object that he has to handle on board his ship at sea in the usual routine of his duties. The beginning and the end of every passage are marked distinctly by work about the ship's anchors. A vessel in the Channel has her anchors always ready, her cables shackled on, and the land almost always in sight. The anchor and the land are indissolubly connected in a sailor's thoughts. But directly she is clear of the narrow seas, heading out into the world with nothing solid to speak of between her and the South Pole, the anchors are got in and the cables disappear from the deck. But the anchors do not disappear. Technically speaking, they are "secured in-board"; and, on the forecastle head, lashed down to ring-bolts with ropes and chains, under the straining sheets of the head-sails, they look very idle and as if asleep. Thus bound, but carefully looked after, inert and powerful, those emblems of hope make company for the look-out man in the night watches; and so the days glide by, with a long rest for those characteristically shaped pieces of iron, reposing forward, visible from almost every part of the ship's deck, waiting for their work on the other side of the world somewhere, while the ship carries them on with a great rush and splutter of foam underneath, and the sprays of the open sea rust their heavy limbs.

The first approach to the land, as yet invisible to the crew's eyes, is announced by the brisk order of the chief mate to the boatswain: "We will get the anchors over this afternoon" or "first thing tomorrow morning," as the case may be. For the chief mate is the keeper of the ship's anchors and the guardian of her cable. There are good ships and bad ships, comfortable ships and ships where, from first day to last of the voyage, there is no rest for a chief mate's body and soul. And ships are what men make them: this is a pronouncement of sailor wisdom, and, no doubt, in the main it is true.

However, there are ships where, as an old grizzled mate once told me, "nothing ever seems to go right!" And, looking from the poop where we both stood (I had paid him a neighborly call in dock), he added: "She's one of them." He glanced up at my face, which expressed a proper professional sympathy, and set me right in my natural surmise: "Oh no; the old man's right enough. He never interferes. Anything that's done in a seamanlike way is good enough for him. And yet, somehow, nothing ever seems to go right in this ship. I tell you what: she is naturally unhandy."

The "old man," of course, was his captain, who just then came on deck in a silk hat and brown overcoat, and, with a civil nod to us, went ashore. He was certainly not more than thirty, and the elderly mate, with a murmur to me of "That's my old man," proceeded to give instances of the natural unhandiness of the ship in a sort of deprecatory tone, as if to say, "You mustn't think I bear a grudge against her for that."

The instances do not matter. The point is that there are ships where things *do* go wrong; but whatever the ship — good or bad, lucky or unlucky — it is in the forepart of her that her chief mate feels most at home. It is emphatically *his* end of the ship, though, of course, he is the executive supervisor of the whole. There are *his* anchors, *his* headgear, his foremast, his station for maneuvering when the captain is in charge. And there, too, live the men, the ship's hands, whom it is his duty to keep employed, fair weather or foul, for the ship's welfare. It is the chief mate, the only figure of the ship's afterguard, who comes bustling forward at the cry of "All hands on deck!" He is the satrap of that province in the autocratic realm of the ship, and more personally responsible for anything that may happen there.

There, too, on the approach to the land, assisted by the boatswain and the carpenter, he "gets the anchors over" with the men of his own watch, whom he knows better than the others. There he sees the cable ranged, the windlass disconnected, the compressors opened; and there, after giving his own last order, "Stand clear of the cable!" he waits attentive, in a silent ship that forges slowly ahead towards her picked-out berth, for the sharp shout from aft, "Let go!" Instantly bending over, he sees the trusty iron fall with a heavy plunge under his eyes, which watch and note whether it has gone clear.

For the anchor "to go clear" means to go clear of its own chain. Your anchor must drop from the bow of your ship with no turn of cable on any of its limbs, else you would be riding to a foul anchor. Unless the pull of the cable is fair on the ring, no anchor can be trusted even on the best of holding ground. In time of stress it is bound to drag, for implements and men must be treated fairly to give you the "virtue" which is in them. The anchor is an emblem of hope, but a foul anchor is worse than the most fallacious of false hopes that ever lured men or nations into a sense of security. And the sense of security, even the most warranted, is a bad councilor. It is the sense which, like that exaggerated feeling of well-being ominous of the coming on of madness, precedes the swift fall of disaster. A seaman laboring under an undue sense of security becomes at once worth hardly half his salt. Therefore, of all my chief officers, the one I trusted most was a man called B———. He had a red moustache, a lean face, also red, and an uneasy eye. He was worth all his salt.

On examining now, after many years, the residue of the feeling which was the outcome of the contact of our personalities, I discover, without much surprise, a certain flavor of dislike. Upon the whole, I think he was one of the most uncomfortable shipmates possible for a young commander. If it is permissible to criticize the absent, I should say he had a little too much of the sense of insecurity which is so invaluable in a seaman. He had an extremely disturbing air of being everlastingly ready (even when seated at table at my right hand before a plate of salt beef) to grapple with some impending calamity. I must hasten to add that he had also the other qualification necessary to make a trustworthy seaman — that of an absolute confidence in himself. What was really wrong with him was that he had these qualities in an unrestful degree. His eternally watchful demeanor, his jerky, nervous talk, even his, as it were, determined silences, seemed to imply — and, I believe, they did imply — that to his mind the ship was never safe in my hands. Such was the man who looked after the anchors of a less than five-hundred-ton barque, my first command, now gone from the face of the earth, but sure of a tenderly remembered existence as long as I live. No anchor could have gone down foul under Mr. B———'s piercing eye. It was good for one to be sure of that when, in an open roadstead, one heard in the cabin the wind pipe up; but still, there were moments when I detested Mr. B——— exceedingly. From the way he used to glare sometimes, I fancy that more than once he paid me back with interest. It so happened that we both loved the little barque very much. And it was just the defect of Mr. B———'s inestimable qualities that he would never persuade himself to believe that the ship was safe in my hands. To begin with, he was more than five years older than myself at a time of life when five years really do count, I being twenty-nine and he thirty-four; then, on our first leaving port (I don't see why I should make a secret of the fact that it was Bangkok), a bit of maneuvering of mine amongst the islands of the Gulf of Siam had given him an unforgettable scare. Ever since then he had nursed in secret a bitter idea of my utter recklessness. But upon the whole, and unless the grip of a man's hand at parting means nothing whatever, I conclude that we did like each other at the end of two years and three months well enough.

The bond between us was the ship; and therein a ship, though she has female attributes and is loved very unreasonably, is different from a woman. That I should have been tremendously smitten with my first command is nothing to wonder at, but I suppose I must admit that Mr. B———'s sentiment was of a higher order. Each of us, of course, was extremely anxious about the good appearance of the beloved object; and, though I was the one to glean compliments ashore, B——— had the more intimate pride of feeling, resembling that of a devoted handmaiden. And that sort of faithful and proud devotion went so far as to make him go about flicking the dust off the varnished teakwood rail of the little craft with a silk pocket handkerchief — a present from Mrs. B———, I believe.

That was the effect of his love for the barque. The effect of his admirable lack of the sense of security once went so far as to make him remark to me: "Well, sir, you *are* a lucky man!"

It was said in a tone full of significance, but not exactly offensive, and it was, I suppose, my innate tact that prevented my asking, "What on earth do you mean by that?"

Later on his meaning was illustrated more fully on a dark night in a tight corner during a dead on-shore gale. I had called him up on deck to help me consider our extremely unpleasant situation. There was not much time for deep thinking, and his summing-up was: "It looks pretty bad, whichever we try; but, then, sir, you always do get out of a mess somehow."

Chapter VI

*I*t is difficult to disconnect the idea of ships' anchors from the idea of the ship's chief mate — the man who sees them go down clear and come up sometimes foul; because not even the most unremitting care can always prevent a ship, swinging to winds and tide, from taking an awkward turn of the cable round stock or fluke. Then the business of "getting the anchor" and securing it afterwards is unduly prolonged, and made a weariness to the chief mate. He is the man who watches the growth of the cable — a sailor's phrase which has all the force, precision, and imagery of technical language that, created by simple men with keen eyes for the real aspect of the things they see in their trade, achieves the just expression seizing upon the essential, which is the ambition of the artist in words. Therefore the sailor will never say, "cast anchor," and the ship-master aft will hail his chief mate on the forecastle in impression-istic phrase: "How does the cable grow?" Because "grow" is the right word for the long drift of a cable emerging aslant under the strain, taut as a bow-string above the water. And it is the voice of the keeper of the ship's anchors that will answer: "Grows right ahead, sir," or "Broad on the bow," or whatever concise and deferential shout will fit the case.

There is no order more noisily given or taken up with lustier shouts on board a homeward-bound merchant ship than the command, "Man the windlass!" The rush of expectant men out of the forecastle, the snatching of hand-spikes, the tramp of feet, the clink of the pawls, make a stirring accompaniment to a plaintive up-anchor song with a roaring chorus; and this burst of noisy activity from a whole ship's crew seems like a voiceful awakening of the ship herself, till then, in the picturesque phrase of Dutch seamen, "lying asleep upon her iron."

For a ship with her sails furled on her squared yards, and reflected from truck to water-line in the smooth gleaming sheet of a landlocked harbor, seems, indeed, to a seaman's eye the most perfect picture of slumbering repose. The getting of your anchor was a noisy operation on board a merchant ship of yesterday — an inspiring, joyous noise, as if, with the emblem of hope, the ship's company expected to drag up out of the depths, each man all his personal hopes into the reach of a securing hand — the hope of home, the hope of rest, of liberty, of dissipation, of hard pleasure, following the hard endurance of many days between sky and water. And this noisiness, this exultation at the moment of the ship's departure, make a tremendous contrast to the silent moments of her arrival in a foreign roadstead — the silent moments when, stripped of her sails, she forges ahead to her chosen berth, the loose canvas fluttering softly in the gear above the heads of the men standing still upon her decks, the master gazing intently forward from the break of the poop. Gradually she loses her way, hardly moving, with the three figures on her forecastle waiting attentively about the cat-head for the last order of, perhaps, full ninety days at sea: "Let go!"

This is the final word of a ship's ended journey, the closing word of her toil and of her achievement. In a life whose worth is told out in passages from port to port, the splash of the anchor's fall and the thunderous rumbling of the chain are like the closing of a distinct period, of which she seems conscious with a slight deep shudder of all her frame. By so much is she nearer to her appointed death, for neither years nor voyages can go on forever. It is to her like the striking of a clock, and in the pause which follows she seems to take count of the passing time.

This is the last important order; the others are mere routine directions. Once more the master is heard: "Give her forty-five fathom to the water's edge," and then he, too, is done for a time. For days he leaves all the harbor work to his chief mate, the keeper of the ship's anchor and of the ship's routine. For days his voice will not be heard raised about the decks, with that curt, austere accent of the man in charge, till, again, when the hatches are on, and in a silent and expectant ship, he shall speak up from aft in commanding tones: "Man the windlass!"

Chapter VII

*T*he other year, looking through a newspaper of sound principles, but whose staff *will* persist in "casting" anchors and going to sea "on" a ship (ough!), I came across an article upon the season's yachting. And, behold! it was a good article. To a man who had but little to do with pleasure sailing (though all sailing is a pleasure), and certainly nothing whatever with racing in open waters, the writer's strictures upon the handicapping of yachts were just intelligible and no more. And I do not pretend to any interest in the enumeration of the great races of that year. As to the 52-foot linear raters, praised so much by the writer, I am warmed up by his approval of their performances; but, as far as any clear conception goes, the descriptive phrase, so precise to the comprehension of a yachtsman, evokes no definite image in my mind.

The writer praises that class of pleasure vessels, and I am willing to endorse his words, as any man who loves every craft afloat would be ready to do. I am disposed to admire and respect the 52-foot linear raters on the word of a man who regrets in such a sympathetic and understanding spirit the threatened decay of yachting seamanship.

Of course, yacht racing is an organized pastime, a function of social idleness ministering to the vanity of certain wealthy inhabitants of these isles nearly as much as to their inborn love of the sea. But the writer of the article in question goes on to point out, with insight and justice, that for a great number of people (20,000, I think he says) it is a means of livelihood — that it is, in his own words, an industry. Now, the moral side of an industry, productive or unproductive, the redeeming and ideal aspect of this bread-winning, is the attainment and preservation of the highest possible skill on the part of the craftsmen. Such skill, the skill of technique, is more than honesty; it is something wider, embracing honesty and grace and rule in an elevated and clear sentiment, not altogether utilitarian, which may be called the honor of labor. It is made up of accumulated tradition, kept alive by individual pride, rendered exact by professional opinion, and, like the higher arts, it spurred on and sustained by discriminating praise.

This is why the attainment of proficiency, the pushing of your skill with attention to the most delicate shades of excellence, is a matter of vital concern. Efficiency of a practically flawless kind may be reached naturally in the struggle for bread. But there is something beyond — a higher point, a subtle and unmistakable touch of love and pride beyond mere skill; almost an inspiration which gives to all work that finish which is almost art — which *is* art.

As men of scrupulous honor set up a high standard of public conscience above the dead-level of an honest community, so men of that skill which passes into art by ceaseless striving raise the dead-level of correct practice in the crafts of land and sea. The conditions fostering the growth of that supreme, alive excellence, as well in work as in play, ought to be preserved with a most careful regard lest the industry or the game should perish of an insidious and inward decay. Therefore I have read with profound regret, in that article upon the yachting season of a certain year, that the seamanship on board racing yachts is not now what it used to be only a few, very few, years ago.

For that was the gist of that article, written evidently by a man who not only knows but *understands* — a thing (let me remark in passing) much rarer than one would expect, because the sort of understanding I mean is inspired by love; and love, though in a sense it may be admitted to be stronger than death, is by no means so universal and so sure. In fact, love is rare — the love of men, of things, of ideas, the love of perfected skill. For love is the enemy of haste; it takes count of passing days, of men who pass away, of a fine art matured slowly in the course of years and doomed in a short time to pass away too, and be no more. Love and regret go hand in hand in this world of changes swifter than the shifting of the clouds reflected in the mirror of the sea.

To penalize a yacht in proportion to the fineness of her performance is unfair to the craft and to her men. It is unfair to the perfection of her form and to the skill of her servants. For we men are, in fact, the servants of our creations. We remain in everlasting bondage to the productions of our brain and to the work of our hands. A man is born to serve his time on this earth, and there is something fine in the service being given on other grounds than that of utility. The bondage of art is very exacting. And, as the writer of the article which started this train of thought says with lovable warmth, the sailing of yachts is a fine art.

His contention is that racing, without time allowances for anything else but tonnage — that is, for size

— has fostered the fine art of sailing to the pitch of perfection. Every sort of demand is made upon the master of a sailing-yacht, and to be penalized in proportion to your success may be of advantage to the sport itself, but it has an obviously deteriorating effect upon the seamanship. The fine art is being lost.

Chapter VIII

*T*he sailing and racing of yachts has developed a class of fore-and-aft sailors, men born and bred to the sea, fishing in winter and yachting in summer; men to whom the handling of that particular rig presents no mystery. It is their striving for victory that has elevated the sailing of pleasure craft to the dignity of a fine art in that special sense. As I have said, I know nothing of racing and but little of fore-and-aft rig; but the advantages of such a rig are obvious, especially for purposes of pleasure, whether in cruising or racing. It requires less effort in handling; the trimming of the sail-planes to the wind can be done with speed and accuracy; the unbroken spread of the sail-area is of infinite advantage; and the greatest possible amount of canvas can be displayed upon the least possible quantity of spars. Lightness and concentrated power are the great qualities of fore-and-aft rig.

A fleet of fore-and-afters at anchor has its own slender graciousness. The setting of their sails resembles more than anything else the unfolding of a bird's wings; the facility of their evolutions is a pleasure to the eye. They are birds of the sea, whose swimming is like flying, and resembles more a natural function than the handling of man-invented appliances. The fore-and-aft rig in its simplicity and the beauty of its aspect under every angle of vision is, I believe, unapproachable. A schooner, yawl, or cutter in charge of a capable man seems to handle herself as if endowed with the power of reasoning and the gift of swift execution. One laughs with sheer pleasure at a smart piece of maneuvering, as at a manifestation of a living creature's quick wit and graceful precision.

Of those three varieties of fore-and-aft rig, the cutter — the racing rig *par excellence* — is of an appearance the most imposing, from the fact that practically all her canvas is in one piece. The enormous mainsail of a cutter, as she draws slowly past a point of land or the end of a jetty under your admiring gaze, invests her with an air of lofty and silent majesty. At anchor a schooner looks better; she has an aspect of greater efficiency and a better balance to the eye, with her two masts distributed over the hull with a swaggering rake aft. The yawl rig one comes in time to love. It is, I should think, the easiest of all to manage.

For racing, a cutter; for a long pleasure voyage, a schooner; for cruising in home waters, the yawl; and the handling of them all is indeed a fine art. It requires not only the knowledge of the general principles of sailing, but a particular acquaintance with the character of the craft. All vessels are handled in the same way as far as theory goes, just as you may deal with all men on broad and rigid principles. But if you want that success in life which comes from the affection and confidence of your fellows, then with no two men, however similar they may appear in their nature, will you deal in the same way. There may be a rule of conduct; there is no rule of human fellowship. To deal with men is as fine an art as it is to deal with ships.

Both men and ships live in an unstable element, are subject to subtle and powerful influences, and want to have their merits understood rather than their faults found out.

It is not what your ship will *not* do that you want to know to get on terms of successful partnership with her; it is, rather, that you ought to have a precise knowledge of what she will do for you when called upon to put forth what is in her by a sympathetic touch. At first sight the difference does not seem great in either line of dealing with the difficult problem of limitations. But the difference is great. The difference lies in the spirit in which the problem is approached. After all, the art of handling ships is finer, perhaps, than the art of handling men.

And, like all fine arts, it must be based upon a broad, solid sincerity, which, like a law of Nature, rules an infinity of different phenomena. Your endeavor must be single-minded. You would talk differently to a coal-heaver and to a professor. But is this duplicity? I deny it. The truth consists in the genuineness of the feeling, in the genuine recognition of the two men, so similar and so different, as your two partners in the hazard of life. Obviously, a humbug, thinking only of winning his little race, would stand a chance of profiting by his artifices. Men, professors or coal-heavers, are easily deceived; they even have an extraordinary knack of lending themselves to deception, a sort of curious and inexplicable propensity to allow themselves to be led by the nose with their eyes open. But a ship is a creature which we have brought into the world, as it were on purpose to keep us up to the mark. In her handling a ship will not put up with a mere pretender, as, for instance, the public will do with Mr. X, the popular statesman, Mr. Y, the popular scientist, or Mr. Z, the popular — what shall we say? — anything from a teacher of high morality to a bagman — who have won their little race. But I would like (though not accustomed to betting) to wager a large sum that not one of the few first-rate skippers of racing yachts has ever been a humbug. It would have been too difficult. The difficulty arises from the fact that one does not deal with ships in a mob, but with a ship as an individual. So we may have to do with men. But in each of us there lurks some particle of the mob spirit, of the mob temperament. No matter how earnestly we strive against each other, we remain brothers on the lowest side of our intellect and in the instability of our feelings. With ships it is not so. Much as they are to us, they are nothing to each other. Those sensitive creatures have no ears for our blandishments. It takes something more than words to cajole them to do our will, to cover us with glory. Luckily, too, or else there would have been more shoddy reputations for first-rate seamanship. Ships have no ears, I repeat, though, indeed, I think I have known ships who really seemed to have had eyes, or else I cannot understand on what ground a certain 1,000-ton barque of my acquaintance on one particular occasion refused to answer her helm, thereby saving a frightful smash to two ships and to a very good man's reputation. I knew her intimately for two years, and in no other instance either before or since have I known her to do that thing. The man she had served so well (guessing, perhaps, at the depths of his affection for her) I have known much longer, and in bare justice to him I must say that this confidence-shattering experience (though so fortunate) only augmented his trust in her. Yes, our ships have no ears, and thus they cannot be deceived. I would illustrate my idea of fidelity as between man and ship, between the master and his art, by a statement which, though it might appear shockingly sophisticated, is really very simple. I would say that a racing-yacht skipper who thought of nothing else but the glory of winning the race would never attain to any eminence of reputation. The genuine masters of their craft — I say this confidently from my experience of ships — have thought of nothing but of doing their very best by the vessel under their charge. To forget one's self, to surrender all personal feeling in the service of that fine art, is the only way for a seaman to the faithful discharge of his trust.

Such is the service of a fine art and of ships that sail the sea. And therein I think I can lay my finger upon the difference between the seamen of yesterday, who are still with us, and the seamen of tomorrow, already entered upon the possession of their inheritance. History repeats itself, but the special call of an art which has passed away is never reproduced. It is as utterly gone out of the world as the song of a destroyed wild bird. Nothing will awaken the same response of pleasurable emotion or conscientious endeavor. And the sailing of any vessel afloat is an art whose fine form seems already receding from us on its way to the overshadowed Valley of Oblivion. The taking of a modern steamship about the world (though one would not minimize its responsibilities) has not the same quality of intimacy with nature, which, after all, is an indispensable condition to the building up of an art. It is less personal and a more exact calling; less arduous, but also less gratifying in the lack of close communion between the artist and the medium of his art. It is, in short, less a matter of love. Its effects are measured exactly in time and space as no effect of an art can be. It is an occupation which a man not desperately subject to sea-sickness can be imagined to follow with content, without enthusiasm, with industry, without affection. Punctuality is its watchword. The incertitude which attends closely every artistic endeavor is absent from its regulated enterprise. It has no great moments of self-confidence, or moments not less great of doubt and heart-searching. It is an industry which, like other industries, has its romance, its honor and its rewards, its bitter anxieties and its hours of ease. But such sea-going has not the artistic quality of a single-handed struggle with something much greater than yourself; it is not the laborious absorbing practice of an art whose ultimate result remains on the knees of the gods. It is not an individual, temperamental achievement, but simply the skilled use of a captured force, merely another step forward upon the way of universal conquest.

Chapter IX

*E*very passage of a ship of yesterday, whose yards were braced round eagerly the very moment the pilot, with his pockets full of letters, had got over the side, was like a race — a race against time, against an ideal standard of achievement outstripping the expectations of common men. Like all true art, the general conduct of a ship and her handling in particular cases had a technique which could be discussed with delight and pleasure by men who found in their work, not bread alone, but an outlet for the peculiarities of their temperament. To get the best and truest effect from the infinitely varying moods of sky and sea, not pictorially, but in the spirit of their calling, was their vocation, one and all; and they recognized this with as much sincerity, and drew as much inspiration from this reality, as any man who ever put brush to canvas. The diversity of temperaments was immense amongst those masters of the fine art.

Some of them were like Royal Academicians of a certain kind. They never startled you by a touch of originality, by a fresh audacity of inspiration. They were safe, very safe. They went about solemnly in the assurance of their consecrated and empty reputation. Names are odious, but I remember one of them who might have been their very president, the P.R.A. of the sea-craft. His weather-beaten and handsome face, his portly presence, his shirt-fronts and broad cuffs and gold links, his air of bluff distinction, impressed the humble beholders (stevedores, tally clerks, tide-waiters) as he walked ashore over the gangway of his ship lying at the Circular Quay in Sydney. His voice was deep, hearty, and authoritative — the voice of a very prince amongst sailors. He did everything with an air which put your attention on the alert and raised your expectations, but the result somehow was always on stereotyped lines, unsuggestive, empty of any lesson that one could lay to heart. He kept his ship in apple-pie order, which would have been seamanlike enough but for a finicking touch in its details. His officers affected a superiority over the rest of us, but the boredom of their souls appeared in their manner of dreary submission to the fads of their commander. It was only his apprenticed boys whose irrepressible spirits were not affected by the solemn and respectable mediocrity of that artist. There were four of these youngsters: one the son of a doctor, another of a colonel, the third of a jeweler; the name of the fourth was Twentyman, and this is all I remember of his parentage. But not one of them seemed to possess the smallest spark of gratitude in his composition. Though their commander was a kind man in his way, and had made a point of introducing them to the best people in the town in order that they should not fall into the bad company of boys belonging to other ships, I regret to say that they made faces at him behind his back, and imitated the dignified carriage of his head without any concealment whatever.

This master of the fine art was a personage and

nothing more; but, as I have said, there was an infinite diversity of temperament amongst the masters of the fine art I have known. Some were great impressionists. They impressed upon you the fear of God and Immensity — or, in other words, the fear of being drowned with every circumstance of terrific grandeur. One may think that the locality of your passing away by means of suffocation in water does not really matter very much. I am not so sure of that. I am, perhaps, unduly sensitive, but I confess that the idea of being suddenly spilt into an infuriated ocean in the midst of darkness and uproar affected me always with a sensation of shrinking distaste. To be drowned in a pond, though it might be called an ignominious fate by the ignorant, is yet a bright and peaceful ending in comparison with some other endings to one's earthly career which I have mentally quaked at in the intervals or even in the midst of violent exertions.

But let that pass. Some of the masters whose influence left a trace upon my character to this very day, combined a fierceness of conception with a certitude of execution upon the basis of just appreciation of means and ends which is the highest quality of the man of action. And an artist is a man of action, whether he creates a personality, invents an expedient, or finds the issue of a complicated situation.

There were masters, too, I have known, whose very art consisted in avoiding every conceivable situation. It is needless to say that they never did great things in their craft; but they were not to be despised for that. They were modest; they understood their limitations. Their own masters had not handed the sacred fire into the keeping of their cold and skillful hands. One of those last I remember specially, now gone to his rest from that sea which his temperament must have made a scene of little more than a peaceful pursuit. Once only did he attempt a stroke of audacity, one early morning, with a steady breeze, entering a crowded roadstead. But he was not genuine in this display which might have been art. He was thinking of his own self; he hankered after the meretricious glory of a showy performance.

As, rounding a dark, wooded point, bathed in fresh air and sunshine, we opened to view a crowd of shipping at anchor lying half a mile ahead of us perhaps, he called me aft from my station on the forecastle head, and, turning over and over his binoculars in his brown hands, said: "Do you see that big, heavy ship with white lower masts? I am going to take up a berth between her and the shore. Now do you see to it that the men jump smartly at the first order."

I answered, "Aye, aye, sir," and verily believed that this would be a fine performance. We dashed on through the fleet in magnificent style. There must have been many open mouths and following eyes on board those ships — Dutch, English, with a sprinkling of Americans and a German or two — who had all hoisted their flags at eight o'clock as if in honor of our arrival. It would have been a fine performance if it had come off, but it did not. Through a touch of self-seeking that modest artist of solid merit became untrue to his temperament. It was not with him art for art's sake: it was art for his own sake; and a dismal failure was the penalty he paid for that greatest of sins. It might have been even heavier, but, as it happened, we did not run our ship ashore, nor did we knock a large hole in the big ship whose lower masts were painted white. But it is a wonder that we did not carry away the cables of both our anchors, for, as may be imagined, I did not stand upon the order to "Let go!" that came to me in a quavering, quite unknown voice from his trembling lips. I let them both go with a celerity which to this day astonishes my memory. No average merchant-man's anchors have ever been let go with such miraculous smartness. And they both held. I could have kissed their rough, cold iron palms in gratitude if they had not been buried in slimy mud under ten fathoms of water. Ultimately they brought us up with the jibboom of a Dutch brig poking through our spanker — nothing worse. And a miss is as good as a mile.

But not in art. Afterwards the master said to me in a shy mumble, "She wouldn't luff up in time, somehow. What's the matter with her?" And I made no answer.

Yet the answer was clear. The ship had found out the momentary weakness of her man. Of all the living creatures upon land and sea, it is ships alone that cannot be taken in by barren pretences, that will not put up with bad art from their masters.

Chapter X

*F*rom the main truck of the average tall ship the horizon describes a circle of many miles, in which you can see another ship right down to her water-line; and these very eyes which follow this writing have counted in their time over a hundred sail becalmed, as if within a magic ring, not very far from the Azores — ships more or less tall. There were hardly two of them heading exactly the same way, as if each had meditated breaking out of the enchanted circle at a different point of the compass. But the spell of the calm is a strong magic. The following day still saw them scattered within sight of each other and heading different ways; but when, at last, the breeze came with the darkling ripple that ran very blue on a pale sea, they all went in the same direction together. For this was the homeward-bound fleet from the far-off ends of the earth, and a Falmouth fruit-schooner, the smallest of them all, was heading the flight. One could have imagined her very fair, if not divinely tall, leaving a scent of lemons and oranges in her wake.

The next day there were very few ships in sight from our mastheads — seven at most, perhaps, with a few more distant specks, hull down, beyond the magic ring of the horizon. The spell of the fair wind has a subtle power to scatter a white-winged company of ships looking all the same way, each with its white fillet of tumbling foam under the bow. It is the calm that brings ships mysteriously together; it is your wind that is the great separator.

The taller the ship, the further she can be seen; and her white tallness breathed upon by the wind first proclaims her size. The tall masts holding aloft the white canvas, spread out like a snare for catching the invisible power of the air, emerge gradually from the water, sail after sail, yard after yard, growing big, till, under the towering structure of her machinery, you perceive the insignificant, tiny speck of her hull.

The tall masts are the pillars supporting the balanced planes that, motionless and silent, catch from the air the ship's motive-power, as it were a gift from Heaven vouchsafed to the audacity of man; and it is the ship's tall spars, stripped and shorn of their white glory, that incline themselves before the anger of the clouded heaven.

When they yield to a squall in a gaunt and naked submission, their tallness is brought best home even to the mind of a seaman. The man who has looked upon his ship going over too far is made aware of the preposterous tallness of a ship's spars. It seems impossible but that those gilt trucks which one had to tilt one's head back to see, now falling into the lower plane of vision, must perforce hit the very edge of the horizon. Such an experience gives you a better impression of the loftiness of your spars than any amount of running aloft could do. And yet in my time the royal yards of an average profitable ship were a good way up above her decks.

No doubt a fair amount of climbing up iron ladders

can be achieved by an active man in a ship's engine-room, but I remember moments when even to my supple limbs and pride of nimbleness the sailing-ship's machinery seemed to reach up to the very stars.

For machinery it is, doing its work in perfect silence and with a motionless grace, that seems to hide a capricious and not always governable power, taking nothing away from the material stores of the earth. Not for it the unerring precision of steel moved by white steam and living by red fire and fed with black coal. The other seems to draw its strength from the very soul of the world, its formidable ally, held to obedience by the frailest bonds, like a fierce ghost captured in a snare of something even finer than spun silk. For what is the array of the strongest ropes, the tallest spars and the stoutest canvas against the mighty breath of the infinite, but thistle stalks, cobwebs and gossamer?

Chapter XI

*I*ndeed, it is less than nothing, and I have seen, when the great soul of the world turned over with a heavy sigh, a perfectly new, extra-stout foresail vanish like a bit of some airy stuff much lighter than gossamer. Then was the time for the tall spars to stand fast in the great uproar. The machinery must do its work even if the soul of the world has gone mad.

The modern steamship advances upon a still and overshadowed sea with a pulsating tremor of her frame, an occasional clang in her depths, as if she had an iron heart in her iron body; with a thudding rhythm in her progress and the regular beat of her propeller, heard afar in the night with an august and plodding sound as of the march of an inevitable future. But in a gale, the silent machinery of a sailing-ship would catch not only the power, but the wild and exulting voice of the world's soul. Whether she ran with her tall spars swinging, or breasted it with her tall spars lying over, there was always that wild song, deep like a chant, for a bass to the shrill pipe of the wind played on the sea-tops, with a punctuating crash, now and then, of a breaking wave. At times the weird effects of that invisible orchestra would get upon a man's nerves till he wished himself deaf.

And this recollection of a personal wish, experienced upon several oceans, where the soul of the world has plenty of room to turn over with a mighty sigh, brings me to the remark that in order to take a proper care of a ship's spars it is just as well for a seaman to have nothing the matter with his ears. Such is the intimacy with which a seaman had to live with his ship of yesterday that his senses were like her senses, that the stress upon his body made him judge of the strain upon the ship's masts.

I had been some time at sea before I became aware of the fact that hearing plays a perceptible part in gauging the force of the wind. It was at night. The ship was one of those iron wool-clippers that the Clyde had floated out in swarms upon the world during the seventh decade of the last century. It was a fine period in ship-building, and also, I might say, a period of overmasting. The spars rigged up on the narrow hulls were indeed tall then, and the ship of which I think, with her colored-glass skylight ends bearing the motto, "Let Glasgow Flourish," was certainly one of the most heavily-sparred specimens. She was built for hard driving, and unquestionably she got all the driving she could stand. Our captain was a man famous for the quick passages he had been used to make in the old Tweed, a ship famous the world over for her speed. The Tweed had been a wooden vessel, and he brought the tradition of quick passages with him into the iron clipper. I was the junior in her, a third mate, keeping watch with the chief officer; and it was just during one of the night watches in a strong, freshening breeze that I overheard two men in a sheltered nook of the main deck exchanging these informing remarks. Said one:

"Should think 'twas time some of them light sails

were coming off her."

And the other, an older man, uttered grumpily: "No fear! not while the chief mate's on deck. He's that deaf he can't tell how much wind there is."

And, indeed, poor P———, quite young, and a smart seaman, was very hard of hearing. At the same time, he had the name of being the very devil of a fellow for carrying on sail on a ship. He was wonderfully clever at concealing his deafness, and, as to carrying on heavily, though he was a fearless man, I don't think that he ever meant to take undue risks. I can never forget his naïve sort of astonishment when remonstrated with for what appeared a most dare-devil performance. The only person, of course, that could remonstrate with telling effect was our captain, himself a man of dare-devil tradition; and really, for me, who knew under whom I was serving, those were impressive scenes. Captain S——— had a great name for sailorlike qualities — the sort of name that compelled my youthful admiration. To this day I preserve his memory, for, indeed, it was he in a sense who completed my training. It was often a stormy process, but let that pass. I am sure he meant well, and I am certain that never, not even at the time, could I bear him malice for his extraordinary gift of incisive criticism. And to hear *him* make a fuss about too much sail on the ship seemed one of those incredible experiences that take place only in one's dreams.

It generally happened in this way: Night, clouds racing overhead, wind howling, royals set, and the ship rushing on in the dark, an immense white sheet of foam level with the lee rail. Mr. P———, in charge of the deck, hooked on to the windward mizzen rigging in a state of perfect serenity; myself, the third mate, also hooked on somewhere to windward of the slanting poop, in a state of the utmost preparedness to jump at the very first hint of some sort of order, but otherwise in a perfectly acquiescent state of mind. Suddenly, out of the companion would appear a tall, dark figure, bareheaded, with a short white beard of a perpendicular cut, very visible in the dark — Captain S———, disturbed in his reading down below by the frightful bounding and lurching of the ship. Leaning very much against the precipitous incline of the deck, he would take a turn or two, perfectly silent, hang on by the compass for a while, take another couple of turns, and suddenly burst out:

"What are you trying to do with the ship?"

And Mr. P———, who was not good at catching what was shouted in the wind, would say interrogatively:

"Yes, sir?"

Then in the increasing gale of the sea there would be a little private ship's storm going on in which you could detect strong language, pronounced in a tone of passion and exculpatory protestations uttered with every possible inflection of injured innocence.

"By Heavens, Mr. P———! I used to carry on sail in my time, but —"

And the rest would be lost to me in a stormy gust of wind.

Then, in a lull, P———'s protesting innocence would become audible:

"She seems to stand it very well."

And then another burst of an indignant voice:

"Any fool can carry sail on a ship —"

And so on and so on, the ship meanwhile rushing on her way with a heavier list, a noisier splutter, a more threatening hiss of the white, almost blinding, sheet of foam to leeward. For the best of it was that Captain S——— seemed constitutionally incapable of giving his officers a definite order to shorten sail; and so that extraordinarily vague row would go on till at last it dawned upon them both, in some particularly alarming gust, that it was time to do something. There is nothing like the fearful inclination of your tall spars overloaded with canvas to bring a deaf man and an angry one to their senses.

Chapter XII

So sail did get shortened more or less in time even in that ship, and her tall spars never went overboard while I served in her. However, all the time I was with them, Captain S——— and Mr. P——— did not get on very well together. If P——— carried on "like the very devil" because he was too deaf to know how much wind there was, Captain S———(who, as I have said, seemed constitutionally incapable of ordering one of his officers to shorten sail) resented the necessity forced upon him by Mr. P———'s desperate goings on. It was in Captain S———'s tradition rather to reprove his officers for not carrying on quite enough — in his phrase "for not taking every ounce of advantage of a fair wind." But there was also a psychological motive that made him extremely difficult to deal with on board that iron clipper. He had just come out of the marvelous Tweed, a ship, I have heard, heavy to look at but of phenomenal speed. In the middle sixties she had beaten by a day and a half the steam mail-boat from Hong Kong to Singapore. There was something peculiarly lucky, perhaps, in the placing of her masts — who knows? Officers of men-of-war used to come on board to take the exact dimensions of her sail-plan. Perhaps there had been a touch of genius or the finger of good fortune in the fashioning of her lines at bow and stern. It is impossible to say. She was built in the East Indies somewhere, of teak-wood throughout, except the deck. She had a great sheer, high bows, and a clumsy stern. The men who had seen her described her to me as "nothing much to look at." But in the great Indian famine of the seventies that ship, already old then, made some wonderful dashes across the Gulf of Bengal with cargoes of rice from Rangoon to Madras.

She took the secret of her speed with her, and, unsightly as she was, her image surely has its glorious place in the mirror of the old sea.

The point, however, is that Captain S———, who used to say frequently, "She never made a decent passage after I left her," seemed to think that the secret of her speed lay in her famous commander. No doubt the secret of many a ship's excellence does lie with the man on board, but it was hopeless for Captain S——— to try to make his new iron clipper equal the feats which made the old Tweed a name of praise upon the lips of English-speaking seamen. There was something pathetic in it, as in the endeavor of an artist in his old age to equal the masterpieces of his youth — for the Tweed's famous passages were Captain S———'s masterpieces. It was pathetic, and perhaps just the least bit dangerous. At any rate, I am glad that, what between Captain S———'s yearning for old triumphs and Mr. P———'s deafness, I have seen some memorable carrying on to make a passage. And I have carried on myself upon the tall spars of that Clyde shipbuilder's masterpiece as I have never carried on in a ship before or since.

The second mate falling ill during the passage, I was promoted to officer of the watch, alone in charge of the deck. Thus the immense leverage of the ship's tall masts became a matter very near my own heart. I suppose it was something of a compliment for a young fellow to be trusted, apparently without any supervision, by such a commander as Captain S——; though, as far as I can remember, neither the tone, nor the manner, nor yet the drift of Captain S——'s remarks addressed to myself did ever, by the most strained interpretation, imply a favorable opinion of my abilities. And he was, I must say, a most uncomfortable commander to get your orders from at night. If I had the watch from eight till midnight, he would leave the deck about nine with the words, "Don't take any sail off her." Then, on the point of disappearing down the companion-way, he would add curtly: "Don't carry anything away." I am glad to say that I never did; one night, however, I was caught, not quite prepared, by a sudden shift of wind.

There was, of course, a good deal of noise — running about, the, shouts of the sailors, the thrashing of the sails — enough, in fact, to wake the dead. But S—— never came on deck. When I was relieved by the chief mate an hour afterwards, he sent for me. I went into his stateroom; he was lying on his couch wrapped up in a rug, with a pillow under his head.

"What was the matter with you up there just now?" he asked.

"Wind flew round on the lee quarter, sir," I said.

"Couldn't you see the shift coming?"

"Yes, sir, I thought it wasn't very far off."

"Why didn't you have your courses hauled up at once, then?" he asked in a tone that ought to have made my blood run cold.

But this was my chance, and I did not let it slip.

"Well, sir," I said in an apologetic tone, "she was going eleven knots very nicely, and I thought she would do for another half-hour or so."

He gazed at me darkly out of his head, lying very still on the white pillow, for a time.

"Ah, yes, another half-hour. That's the way ships get dismasted."

And that was all I got in the way of a wigging. I waited a little while and then went out, shutting carefully the door of the state-room after me.

Well, I have loved, lived with, and left the sea without ever seeing a ship's tall fabric of sticks, cobwebs and gossamer go by the board. Sheer good luck, no doubt. But as to poor P———, I am sure that he would not have got off scot-free like this but for the god of gales, who called him away early from this earth, which is three parts ocean, and therefore a fit abode for sailors. A few years afterwards I met in an Indian port a man who had served in the ships of the same company. Names came up in our talk, names of our colleagues in the same employ, and, naturally enough, I asked after P———. Had he got a command yet? And the other man answered carelessly:

"No; but he's provided for, anyhow. A heavy sea took him off the poop in the run between New Zealand and the Horn."

Thus P——— passed away from amongst the tall spars of ships that he had tried to their utmost in many a spell of boisterous weather. He had shown me what carrying on meant, but he was not a man to learn discretion from. He could not help his deafness. One can only remember his cheery temper, his admiration for the jokes in *Punch*, his little oddities — like his strange passion for borrowing looking-glasses, for instance. Each of our cabins had its own looking-glass screwed to the bulkhead, and what he wanted with more of them we never could fathom. He asked for the loan in confidential tones. Why? Mystery. We made various surmises. No one will ever know now. At any rate, it was a harmless eccentricity, and may the god of gales, who took him away so abruptly between New Zealand and the Horn, let his soul rest in some Paradise of true seamen, where no amount of carrying on will ever dismast a ship!

Chapter XIII

*T*here has been a time when a ship's chief mate, pocketbook in hand and pencil behind his ear, kept one eye aloft upon his riggers and the other down the hatchway on the stevedores, and watched the disposition of his ship's cargo, knowing that even before she started he was already doing his best to secure for her an easy and quick passage.

The hurry of the times, the loading and discharging organization of the docks, the use of hoisting machinery which works quickly and will not wait, the cry for prompt dispatch, the very size of his ship, stand nowadays between the modern seaman and the thorough knowledge of his craft.

There are profitable ships and unprofitable ships. The profitable ship will carry a large load through all the hazards of the weather, and, when at rest, will stand up in dock and shift from berth to berth without ballast. There is a point of perfection in a ship as a worker when she is spoken of as being able to *sail* without ballast. I have never met that sort of paragon myself, but I have seen these paragons advertised amongst ships for sale. Such excess of virtue and good nature on the part of a ship always provoked my mistrust. It is open to any man to say that his ship will sail without ballast; and he will say it, too, with every mark of profound conviction, especially if he is not going to sail in her himself. The risk of advertising her as able to sail without ballast is not great, since the statement does not imply a warranty of her arriving anywhere. Moreover, it is strictly true that most ships will sail without ballast for some little time before they turn turtle upon the crew.

A ship owner loves a profitable ship; the seaman is proud of her; a doubt of her good looks seldom exists in his mind; but if he can boast of her more useful qualities it is an added satisfaction for his self-love.

The loading of ships was once a matter of skill, judgment, and knowledge. Thick books have been written about it. "Stevens on Stowage" is a portly volume with the renown and weight (in its own world) of Coke on Littleton. Stevens is an agreeable writer, and, as is the case with men of talent, his gifts adorn his sterling soundness. He gives you the official teaching on the whole subject, is precise as to rules, mentions illustrative events, quotes law cases where verdicts turned upon a point of stowage. He is never pedantic, and, for all his close adherence to broad principles, he is ready to admit that no two ships can be treated exactly alike.

Stevedoring, which had been a skilled labor, is fast becoming a labor without the skill. The modern steamship with her many holds is not loaded within the sailorlike meaning of the word. She is filled up. Her cargo is not stowed in any sense; it is simply dumped into her through six hatchways, more or less, by twelve winches or so, with clatter and hurry and racket and heat, in a cloud of steam and a mess of coal-dust. As long as you keep her propeller under water and take care, say, not to fling down barrels of oil on top of bales of silk, or deposit an iron bridge-girder of five ton or so upon a bed of coffee-bags, you have done about all in the way of duty that the cry for prompt dispatch will allow you to do.

Chapter XIV

*T*he sailing-ship, when I knew her in her days of perfection, was a sensible creature. When I say her days of perfection, I mean perfection of build, gear, seaworthy qualities and case of handling, not the perfection of speed. That quality has departed with the change of building material. No iron ship of yesterday ever attained the marvels of speed which the seamanship of men famous in their time had obtained from their wooden, copper-sheeted predecessors. Everything had been done to make the iron ship perfect, but no wit of man had managed to devise an efficient coating composition to keep her bottom clean with the smooth cleanness of yellow metal sheeting. After a spell of a few weeks at sea, an iron ship begins to lag as if she had grown tired too soon. It is only her bottom that is getting foul. A very little affects the speed of an iron ship which is not driven on by a merciless propeller. Often it is impossible to tell what inconsiderate trifle puts her off her stride. A certain mysteriousness hangs around the quality of speed as it was displayed by the old sailing-ships commanded by a competent seaman. In those days the speed depended upon the seaman;

therefore, apart from the laws, rules, and regulations for the good preservation of his cargo, he was careful of his loading, — or what is technically called the trim of his ship. Some ships sailed fast on an even keel, others had to be trimmed quite one foot by the stern, and I have heard of a ship that gave her best speed on a wind when so loaded as to float a couple of inches by the head.

I call to mind a winter landscape in Amsterdam — a flat foreground of waste land, with here and there stacks of timber, like the huts of a camp of some very miserable tribe; the long stretch of the Handelskade; cold, stone-faced quays, with the snow-sprinkled ground and the hard, frozen water of the canal, in which were set ships one behind another with their frosty mooring-ropes hanging slack and their decks idle and deserted, because, as the master stevedore (a gentle, pale person, with a few golden hairs on his chin and a reddened nose) informed me, their cargoes were frozen-in up-country on barges and schuyts. In the distance, beyond the waste ground, and running parallel with the line of ships, a line of brown, warm-toned houses seemed bowed under snow-laden roofs. From afar at the end of Tsar Peter Straat, issued in the frosty air the tinkle of bells of the horse tramcars, appearing and disappearing in the opening between the buildings, like little toy carriages harnessed with toy horses and played with by people that appeared no bigger than children.

I was, as the French say, biting my fists with impatience for that cargo frozen up-country; with rage at that canal set fast, at the wintry and deserted aspect of all those ships that seemed to decay in grim depression for want of the open water. I was chief mate, and very much alone. Directly I had joined I received from my owners instructions to send all the ship's apprentices away on leave together, because in such weather there was nothing for anybody to do, unless to keep up a fire in the cabin stove. That was attended to by a snuffy and mop-headed, inconceivably dirty, and weirdly toothless Dutch ship-keeper, who could hardly speak three words of English, but who must have had some considerable knowledge of the language, since he managed invariably to interpret in the contrary sense everything that was said to him.

Notwithstanding the little iron stove, the ink froze on the swing-table in the cabin, and I found it more convenient to go ashore stumbling over the arctic waste-land and shivering in glazed tramcars in order to write my evening letter to my owners in a gorgeous café in the center of the town. It was an immense place, lofty and gilt, upholstered in red plush, full of electric lights and so thoroughly warmed that even the marble tables felt tepid to the touch. The waiter who brought me my cup of coffee bore, by comparison with my utter isolation, the dear aspect of an intimate friend. There, alone in a noisy crowd, I would write slowly a letter addressed to Glasgow, of which the gist would be: There is no cargo, and no prospect of any coming till late spring apparently. And all the time I sat there the necessity of getting back to the ship bore heavily on my already half-congealed spirits — the shivering in glazed tramcars, the stumbling over the snow-sprinkled waste ground, the vision of ships frozen in a row, appearing vaguely like corpses of black vessels in a white world, so silent, so lifeless, so soulless they seemed to be.

With precaution I would go up the side of my own particular corpse, and would feel her as cold as ice itself and as slippery under my feet. My cold berth would swallow up like a chilly burial niche my bodily shivers and my mental excitement. It was a cruel winter. The very air seemed as hard and trenchant as steel; but it would have taken much more than this to extinguish my sacred fire for the exercise of my craft. No young man of twenty-four appointed chief mate for the first time in his life would have let that Dutch tenacious winter penetrate into his heart. I think that in those days I never forgot the fact of my elevation for five consecutive minutes. I fancy it kept me warm, even in my slumbers, better than the high pile of blankets, which positively crackled with frost as I threw them off in the morning. And I would get up early for no reason whatever except that I was in sole charge. The new captain had not been appointed yet.

Almost each morning a letter from my owners would arrive, directing me to go to the charterers and clamor for the ship's cargo; to threaten them with the heaviest penalties of demurrage; to demand that this assortment of varied merchandise, set fast in a landscape of ice and windmills somewhere up-country, should be put on rail instantly, and fed up to the ship in regular quantities everyday. After drinking some hot coffee, like an Arctic explorer setting off on a sledge journey towards the North Pole, I would go ashore and roll shivering in a tramcar into the very heart of the town, past clean-faced houses, past thousands of brass knockers upon a thousand painted doors glimmering behind rows of trees of the pavement species, leafless, gaunt, seemingly dead forever.

That part of the expedition was easy enough, though the horses were painfully glistening with icicles, and the aspect of the tram-conductors' faces presented a repulsive blending of crimson and purple. But as to frightening or bullying, or even wheedling some sort of answer out of Mr. Hudig, that was another matter altogether. He was a big, swarthy Netherlander, with black moustaches and a bold glance. He always began by shoving me into a chair before I had time to open my mouth, gave me cordially a large cigar, and in excellent English would start to talk everlastingly about the phenomenal severity of the weather. It was impossible to threaten a man who, though he possessed the language perfectly, seemed incapable of understanding any phrase pronounced in a tone of remonstrance or discontent. As to quarreling with him, it would have been stupid. The weather was too bitter for that. His office was so warm, his fire so bright, his sides shook so heartily with laughter, that I experienced always a great difficulty in making up my mind to reach for my hat.

At last the cargo did come. At first it came dribbling in by rail in trucks, till the thaw set in; and then fast, in a multitude of barges, with a great rush of unbound waters. The gentle master stevedore had his hands very full at last; and the chief mate became worried in his mind as to the proper distribution of the weight of his first cargo in a ship he did not personally know before.

Ships do want humoring. They want humoring in handling; and if you mean to handle them well, they must have been humored in the distribution of the weight which you ask them to carry through the good and evil fortune of a passage. Your ship is a tender creature, whose idiosyncrasies must be attended to if you mean her to come with credit to herself and you through the rough-and-tumble of her life.

Chapter XV

So seemed to think the new captain, who arrived the day after we had finished loading, on the very eve of the day of sailing. I first beheld him on the quay, a complete stranger to me, obviously not a Hollander, in a black bowler and a short drab overcoat, ridiculously out of tone with the winter aspect of the wastelands, bordered by the brown fronts of houses with their roofs dripping with melting snow.

This stranger was walking up and down absorbed in the marked contemplation of the ship's fore and aft trim; but when I saw him squat on his heels in the slush at the very edge of the quay to peer at the draught of water under her counter, I said to myself, "This is the captain." And presently I descried his luggage coming along — a real sailor's chest, carried by means of rope-beckets between two men, with a couple of leather portmanteaus and a roll of charts sheeted in canvas piled upon the lid. The sudden, spontaneous agility with which he bounded aboard right off the rail afforded me the first glimpse of his real character. Without further preliminaries than a friendly nod, he addressed me: "You have got her pretty well in her fore and aft trim. Now, what about your weights?"

I told him I had managed to keep the weight suffi-ciently well up, as I thought, one-third of the whole being in the upper part "above the beams," as the technical expression has it. He whistled "Phew!" scru-tinizing me from head to foot. A sort of smiling vexation was visible on his ruddy face.

"Well, we shall have a lively time of it this passage, I bet," he said.

He knew. It turned out he had been chief mate of her for the two preceding voyages; and I was already familiar with his handwriting in the old log-books I had been perusing in my cabin with a natural curiosity, looking up the records of my new ship's luck, of her behavior, of the good times she had had, and of the troubles she had escaped.

He was right in his prophecy. On our passage from Amsterdam to Samarang with a general cargo, of which, alas! only one-third in weight was stowed "above the beams," we had a lively time of it. It was lively, but not joyful. There was not even a single moment of comfort in it, because no seaman can feel comfortable in body or mind when he has made his ship uneasy.

To travel along with a cranky ship for ninety days or so is no doubt a nerve-trying experience; but in this case what was wrong with our craft was this: that by my system of loading she had been made much too stable.

Neither before nor since have I felt a ship roll so abruptly, so violently, so heavily. Once she began, you felt that she would never stop, and this hopeless sen-sation, characterizing the motion of ships whose center of gravity is brought down too low in loading, made everyone on board weary of keeping on his feet. I remember once overhearing one of the hands say: "By Heavens, Jack! I feel as if I didn't mind how soon I let myself go, and let the blamed hooker knock my brains out if she likes." The captain used to remark frequently: "Ah, yes; I dare say one-third weight above beams would have been quite enough for most ships. But then, you see, there's no two of them alike on the seas, and she's an uncommonly ticklish jade to load."

Down south, running before the gales of high latitudes, she made our life a burden to us. There were days when nothing would keep even on the swing-tables, when there was no position where you could fix yourself so as not to feel a constant strain upon all the muscles of your body. She rolled and rolled with an awful dislodging jerk and that dizzily fast sweep of her masts on every swing. It was a wonder that the men sent aloft were not flung off the yards, the yards not flung off the masts, the masts not flung overboard. The captain in his armchair, holding on grimly at the head of the table, with the soup-tureen rolling on one side of the cabin and the steward sprawling on the other, would observe, looking at me: "That's your one-third above the beams. The only thing that surprises me is that the sticks have stuck to her all this time."

Ultimately some of the minor spars did go — nothing important: spanker-booms and suchlike — because at times the frightful impetus of her rolling would part a fourfold tackle of new three-inch Manila line as if it were weaker than pack-thread.

It was only poetic justice that the chief mate who had made a mistake — perhaps a half-excusable one — about the distribution of his ship's cargo should pay the penalty. A piece of one of the minor spars that did carry away flew against the chief mate's back, and sent him sliding on his face for quite a considerable distance along the main deck. Thereupon followed various and unpleasant consequences of a physical order — "queer symptoms," as the captain, who treated them, used to say; inexplicable periods of powerlessness, sudden accesses of mysterious pain; and the patient agreed fully with the regretful mutters of his very attentive captain wishing that it had been a straightforward broken leg. Even the Dutch doctor who took the case up in Samarang offered no scientific explanation. All he said was: "Ah, friend, you are young yet; it may be very serious for your whole life. You must leave your ship; you must quite silent be for three months — quite silent."

Of course, he meant the chief mate to keep quiet — to lay up, as a matter of fact. His manner was impressive enough, if his English was childishly imperfect when compared with the fluency of Mr. Hudig, the figure at the other end of that passage, and memorable enough in its way. In a great airy ward of a Far Eastern hospital, lying on my back, I had plenty of leisure to remember the dreadful cold and snow of Amsterdam, while looking at the fronds of the palm trees tossing and rustling at the height of the window. I could remember the elated feeling and the soul-gripping cold of those tramway journeys taken into town to put what in diplomatic language is called pressure upon the good Hudig, with his warm fire, his armchair, his big cigar, and the never-failing suggestion in his good-natured voice: "I suppose in the end it is you they will appoint captain before the ship sails?" It may have been his extreme good nature, the serious, unsmiling good nature of a fat, swarthy man with coal-black moustache and steady eyes; but he might have been a bit of a diplomatist, too. His enticing suggestions I used to repel modestly by the assurance that it was extremely unlikely, as I had not enough experience. "You know very well how to go about business matters," he used to say, with a sort of affected moodiness clouding his serene round face. I wonder whether he ever laughed to himself after I had left the office. I dare say he never did, because I understand that diplomatists, in and out of the career, take themselves and their tricks with an exemplary seriousness.

But he had nearly persuaded me that I was fit in every way to be trusted with a command. There came three months of mental worry, hard rolling, remorse, and physical pain to drive home the lesson of insufficient experience.

Yes, your ship wants to be humored with knowledge. You must treat with an understanding consideration the mysteries of her feminine nature, and then she will stand by you faithfully in the unceasing struggle with forces wherein defeat is no shame. It is a serious relation, that in which a man stands to his ship. She has her rights as though she could breathe and speak; and, indeed, there are ships that, for the right man, will do anything but speak, as the saying goes.

A ship is not a slave. You must make her easy in a seaway, you must never forget that you owe her the fullest share of your thought, of your skill, of your self-love. If you remember that obligation, naturally and without effort, as if it were an instinctive feeling of your inner life, she will sail, stay, run for you as long as she is able, or, like a sea-bird going to rest upon the angry waves, she will lay out the heaviest gale that ever made you doubt living long enough to see another sunrise.

Chapter XVI

*O*ften I turn with melancholy eagerness to the space reserved in the newspapers under the general heading of "Shipping Intelligence." I meet there the names of ships I have known. Every year some of these names disappear — the names of old friends. "Tempi passati!"

The different divisions of that kind of news are set down in their order, which varies but slightly in its arrangement of concise headlines. And first comes "Speakings" — reports of ships met and signaled at sea, name, port, where from, where bound for, so many days out, ending frequently with the words "All well." Then come "Wrecks and Casualties" — a longish array of paragraphs, unless the weather has been fair and clear, and friendly to ships all over the world.

On some days there appears the heading "Overdue" — an ominous threat of loss and sorrow trembling yet in the balance of fate. There is something sinister to a seaman in the very grouping of the letters which form this word, clear in its meaning, and seldom threatening in vain.

Only a very few days more — appallingly few to the hearts which had set themselves bravely to hope against hope — three weeks, a month later, perhaps, the name of ships under the blight of the "Overdue" heading shall appear again in the column of "Shipping Intelligence," but under the final declaration of "Missing."

"The ship, or barque, or brig So-and-so, bound from such a port, with such and such cargo, for such another port, having left at such and such a date, last spoken at sea on such a day, and never having been heard of since, was posted today as missing." Such in its strictly official eloquence is the form of funeral orations on ships that, perhaps wearied with a long struggle, or in some unguarded moment that may come to the readiest of us, had let themselves be overwhelmed by a sudden blow from the enemy.

Who can say? Perhaps the men she carried had asked her to do too much, had stretched beyond breaking-point the enduring faithfulness which seems wrought and hammered into that assemblage of iron ribs and plating, of wood and steel and canvas and wire, which goes to the making of a ship — a complete creation endowed with character, individuality, qualities and defects, by men whose hands launch her upon the water, and that other men shall learn to know with an intimacy surpassing the intimacy of man with man, to love with a love nearly as great as that of man for woman, and often as blind in its infatuated disregard of defects.

There are ships which bear a bad name, but I have yet to meet one whose crew for the time being failed to stand up angrily for her against every criticism. One ship which I call to mind now had the reputation of killing somebody every voyage she made. This was no calumny, and yet I remember well, somewhere far back in the late seventies, that the crew of that ship were, if anything, rather proud of her evil fame, as if they had been an utterly corrupt lot of desperadoes glorying in their association with an atrocious creature. We, belonging to other vessels moored all about the Circular Quay in Sydney, used to shake our heads at her with a great sense of the unblemished virtue of our own well-loved ships.

I shall not pronounce her name. She is "missing" now, after a sinister but, from the point of view of her owners, a useful career extending over many years, and, I should say, across every ocean of our globe. Having killed a man for every voyage, and perhaps rendered more misanthropic by the infirmities that come with years upon a ship, she had made up her mind to kill all hands at once before leaving the scene of her exploits. A fitting end, this, to a life of usefulness and crime — in a last outburst of an evil passion supremely satisfied on some wild night, perhaps, to the applauding clamor of wind and wave.

How did she do it? In the word "missing" there is a horrible depth of doubt and speculation. Did she go quickly from under the men's feet, or did she resist to the end, letting the sea batter her to pieces, start her butts, wrench her frame, load her with an increasing weight of salt water, and, dismasted, unmanageable, rolling heavily, her boats gone, her decks swept, had she wearied her men half to death with the unceasing labor at the pumps before she sank with them like a stone?

However, such a case must be rare. I imagine a raft of some sort could always be contrived; and, even if it saved no one, it would float on and be picked up, perhaps conveying some hint of the vanished name. Then that ship would not be, properly speaking, missing. She would be "lost with all hands," and in that distinction there is a subtle difference — less horror and a less appalling darkness.

Chapter XVII

*T*he unholy fascination of dread dwells in the thought of the last moments of a ship reported as "missing" in the columns of the *Shipping Gazette*. Nothing of her ever comes to light — no grating, no lifebuoy, no piece of boat or branded oar — to give a hint of the place and date of her sudden end. The *Shipping Gazette* does not even call her "lost with all hands." She remains simply "missing"; she has disappeared enigmatically into a mystery of fate as big as the world, where your imagination of a brother-sailor, of a fellow-servant and lover of ships, may range unchecked.

And yet sometimes one gets a hint of what the last scene may be like in the life of a ship and her crew, which resembles a drama in its struggle against a great force bearing it up, formless, ungraspable, chaotic and mysterious, as fate.

It was on a gray afternoon in the lull of a three days' gale that had left the Southern Ocean tumbling heavily upon our ship, under a sky hung with rags of clouds that seemed to have been cut and hacked by the keen edge of a sou'-west gale.

Our craft, a Clyde-built barque of 1,000 tons, rolled

so heavily that something aloft had carried away. No matter what the damage was, but it was serious enough to induce me to go aloft myself with a couple of hands and the carpenter to see the temporary repairs properly done.

Sometimes we had to drop everything and cling with both hands to the swaying spars, holding our breath in fear of a terribly heavy roll. And, wallowing as if she meant to turn over with us, the barque, her decks full of water, her gear flying in bights, ran at some ten knots an hour. We had been driven far south — much farther that way than we had meant to go; and suddenly, up there in the slings of the foreyard, in the midst of our work, I felt my shoulder gripped with such force in the carpenter's powerful paw that I positively yelled with unexpected pain. The man's eyes stared close in my face, and he shouted, "Look, sir! look! What's this?" pointing ahead with his other hand.

At first I saw nothing. The sea was one empty wilderness of black and white hills. Suddenly, half-concealed in the tumult of the foaming rollers I made out awash, something enormous, rising and falling — something spread out like a burst of foam, but with a more bluish, more solid look.

It was a piece of an ice-floe melted down to a fragment, but still big enough to sink a ship, and floating lower than any raft, right in our way, as if ambushed among the waves with murderous intent. There was no time to get down on deck. I shouted from aloft till my head was ready to split. I was heard aft, and we managed to clear the sunken floe which had come all the way from the Southern ice-cap to have a try at our unsuspecting lives. Had it been an hour later, nothing could have saved the ship, for no eye could have made out in the dusk that pale piece of ice swept over by the white-crested waves.

And as we stood near the taffrail side by side, my captain and I, looking at it, hardly discernible already, but still quite close-to on our quarter, he remarked in a meditative tone:

"But for the turn of that wheel just in time, there would have been another case of a 'missing' ship."

Nobody ever comes back from a "missing" ship to tell how hard was the death of the craft, and how sudden and overwhelming the last anguish of her men. Nobody can say with what thoughts, with what regrets, with what words on their lips they died. But there is something fine in the sudden passing away of these hearts from the extremity of struggle and stress and tremendous uproar — from the vast, unrestful rage of the surface to the profound peace of the depths, sleeping untroubled since the beginning of ages.

Chapter XVIII

*B*ut if the word "missing" brings all hope to an end and settles the loss of the underwriters, the word "overdue" confirms the fears already born in many homes ashore, and opens the door of speculation in the market of risks.

Maritime risks, be it understood. There is a class of optimists ready to reinsure an "overdue" ship at a heavy premium. But nothing can insure the hearts on shore against the bitterness of waiting for the worst.

For if a "missing" ship has never turned up within the memory of seamen of my generation, the name of an "overdue" ship, trembling as it were on the edge of the fatal heading, has been known to appear as "arrived."

It must blaze up, indeed, with a great brilliance the dull printer's ink expended on the assemblage of the few letters that form the ship's name to the anxious eyes scanning the page in fear and trembling. It is like the message of reprieve from the sentence of sorrow suspended over many a home, even if some of the men in her have been the most homeless mortals that you may find among the wanderers of the sea.

The reinsurer, the optimist of ill-luck and disaster, slaps his pocket with satisfaction. The underwriter, who had been trying to minimize the amount of impending loss, regrets his premature pessimism. The ship has been stauncher, the skies more merciful, the seas less angry, or perhaps the men on board of a finer temper than he has been willing to take for granted.

"The ship So-and-so, bound to such a port, and posted as 'overdue,' has been reported yesterday as having arrived safely at her destination."

Thus run the official words of the reprieve addressed to the hearts ashore lying under a heavy sentence. And they come swiftly from the other side of the earth, over wires and cables, for your electric telegraph is a great alleviator of anxiety. Details, of course, shall follow. And they may unfold a tale of narrow escape, of steady ill-luck, of high winds and heavy weather, of ice, of interminable calms or endless head-gales; a tale of difficulties overcome, of adversity defied by a small knot of men upon the great loneliness of the sea; a tale of resource, of courage — of helplessness, perhaps.

Of all ships disabled at sea, a steamer who has lost her propeller is the most helpless. And if she drifts into an unpopulated part of the ocean she may soon become overdue. The menace of the "overdue" and the finality of "missing" come very quickly to steamers whose life, fed on coals and breathing the black breath of smoke into the air, goes on in disregard of wind and wave. Such a one, a big steamship, too, whose working life had been a record of faithful keeping time from land to land, in disregard of wind and sea, once lost her propeller down south, on her passage out to New Zealand.

It was the wintry, murky time of cold gales and heavy seas. With the snapping of her tail-shaft her life seemed suddenly to depart from her big body, and from a stubborn, arrogant existence she passed all at once into the passive state of a drifting log. A ship sick with her own weakness has not the pathos of a ship vanquished in a battle with the elements, wherein consists the inner drama of her life. No seaman can look without compassion upon a disabled ship, but to look at a sailing-vessel with her lofty spars gone is to look upon a defeated but indomitable warrior. There is defiance in the remaining stumps of her masts, raised up like maimed limbs against the menacing scowl of a stormy sky; there is high courage in the upward sweep of her lines towards the bow; and as soon as, on a hastily-rigged spar, a strip of canvas is shown to the wind to keep her head to sea, she faces the waves again with an unsubdued courage.

Chapter XIX

*T*he efficiency of a steamship consists not so much in her courage as in the power she carries within herself. It beats and throbs like a pulsating heart within her iron ribs, and when it stops, the steamer, whose life is not so much a contest as the disdainful ignoring of the sea, sickens and dies upon the waves. The sailing-ship, with her unthrobbing body, seemed to lead mysteriously a sort of unearthly existence, bordering upon the magic of the invisible forces, sustained by the inspiration of life-giving and death-dealing winds.

So that big steamer, dying by a sudden stroke, drifted, an unwieldy corpse, away from the track of other ships. And she would have been posted really as "overdue," or maybe as "missing," had she not been sighted in a snowstorm, vaguely, like a strange rolling island, by a whaler going north from her Polar cruising ground. There was plenty of food on board, and I don't know whether the nerves of her passengers were at all affected by anything else than the sense of interminable boredom or the vague fear of that unusual situation. Does a passenger ever feel the life of the ship in which he is being carried like a sort of honored bale of highly sensitive goods? For a man who has never been a passenger it is impossible to say. But I know that there is no harder trial for a seaman than to feel a dead ship under his feet.

There is no mistaking that sensation, so dismal, so tormenting and so subtle, so full of unhappiness and unrest. I could imagine no worse eternal punishment for evil seamen who die unrepentant upon the earthly sea than that their souls should be condemned to man the ghosts of disabled ships, drifting forever across a ghostly and tempestuous ocean.

She must have looked ghostly enough, that broken-down steamer, rolling in that snowstorm — a dark apparition in a world of white snowflakes to the staring eyes of that whaler's crew. Evidently they didn't believe in ghosts, for on arrival into port her captain unro-mantically reported having sighted a disabled steamer in latitude somewhere about 50 degrees S. and a longi-tude still more uncertain. Other steamers came out to look for her, and ultimately towed her away from the cold edge of the world into a harbor with docks and workshops, where, with many blows of hammers, her pulsating heart of steel was set going again to go forth presently in the renewed pride of its strength, fed on fire and water, breathing black smoke into the air, pulsating, throbbing, shouldering its arrogant way against the great rollers in blind disdain of winds and sea.

The track she had made when drifting while her heart stood still within her iron ribs looked like a tangled thread on the white paper of the chart. It was shown to me by a friend, her second officer. In that surprising tangle there were words in minute letters — "gales," "thick fog," "ice" — written by him here and there as memoranda of the weather. She had intermi-nably turned upon her tracks, she had crossed and recrossed her haphazard path till it resembled nothing so much as a puzzling maze of penciled lines without a meaning. But in that maze there lurked all the romance of the "overdue" and a menacing hint of "missing."

"We had three weeks of it," said my friend, "just think of that!"

"How did you feel about it?" I asked.

He waved his hand as much as to say: It's all in the day's work. But then, abruptly, as if making up his mind:

"I'll tell you. Towards the last I used to shut myself up in my berth and cry."

"Cry?"

"Shed tears," he explained briefly, and rolled up the chart.

I can answer for it, he was a good man — as good as ever stepped upon a ship's deck — but he could not bear the feeling of a dead ship under his feet: the sickly, disheartening feeling which the men of some "overdue" ships that come into harbor at last under a jury-rig must have felt, combated, and overcome in the faithful discharge of their duty.

Chapter XX

*I*t is difficult for a seaman to believe that his stranded ship does not feel as unhappy at the unnatural predicament of having no water under her keel as he is himself at feeling her stranded.

Stranding is, indeed, the reverse of sinking. The sea does not close upon the water-logged hull with a sunny ripple, or maybe with the angry rush of a curling wave, erasing her name from the roll of living ships. No. It is as if an invisible hand had been stealthily uplifted from the bottom to catch hold of her keel as it glides through the water.

More than any other event does stranding bring to the sailor a sense of utter and dismal failure. There are strandings and strandings, but I am safe to say that 90 per cent. of them are occasions in which a sailor, without dishonor, may well wish himself dead; and I have no doubt that of those who had the experience of their ship taking the ground, 90 per cent. did actually for five seconds or so wish themselves dead.

"Taking the ground" is the professional expression for a ship that is stranded in gentle circumstances. But the feeling is more as if the ground had taken hold of her. It is for those on her deck a surprising sensation. It is as if your feet had been caught in an imponderable snare; you feel the balance of your body threatened, and the steady poise of your mind is destroyed at once. This sensation lasts only a second, for even while you stagger something seems to turn over in your head, bringing uppermost the mental exclamation, full of astonishment and dismay, "By Jove! she's on the ground!"

And that is very terrible. After all, the only mission of a seaman's calling is to keep ships' keels off the ground. Thus the moment of her stranding takes away from him every excuse for his continued existence. To keep ships afloat is his business; it is his trust; it is the effective formula of the bottom of all these vague impulses, dreams, and illusions that go to the making up of a boy's vocation. The grip of the land upon the keel of your ship, even if nothing worse comes of it than the wear and tear of tackle and the loss of time, remains in a seaman's memory an indelibly fixed taste of disaster.

"Stranded" within the meaning of this paper stands for a more or less excusable mistake. A ship may be "driven ashore" by stress of weather. It is a catastrophe, a defeat. To be "run ashore" has the littleness, poignancy, and bitterness of human error.

Chapter XXI

*T*hat is why your "strandings" are for the most part so unexpected. In fact, they are all unexpected, except those heralded by some short glimpse of the danger, full of agitation and excitement, like an awakening from a dream of incredible folly.

The land suddenly at night looms up right over your bows, or perhaps the cry of "Broken water ahead!" is raised, and some long mistake, some complicated edifice of self-delusion, overconfidence, and wrong reasoning is brought down in a fatal shock, and the heart-searing experience of your ship's keel scraping and scrunching over, say, a coral reef. It is a sound, for its size, far more terrific to your soul than that of a world coming violently to an end. But out of that chaos your belief in your own prudence and sagacity reasserts itself. You ask yourself, Where on earth did I get to? How on earth did I get there? with a conviction that it could not be your own act, that there has been at work some mysterious conspiracy of accident; that the charts are all wrong, and if the charts are not wrong, that land and sea have changed their places; that your misfortune shall forever remain inexplicable, since you have lived always with the sense of your trust, the last thing on closing your eyes, the first on opening them, as if your mind had kept firm hold of your responsibility during the hours of sleep.

You contemplate mentally your mischance, till little by little your mood changes, cold doubt steals into the very marrow of your bones, you see the inexplicable fact in another light. That is the time when you ask yourself, How on earth could I have been fool enough to get there? And you are ready to renounce all belief in your good sense, in your knowledge, in your fidelity, in what you thought till then was the best in you, giving you the daily bread of life and the moral support of other men's confidence.

The ship is lost or not lost. Once stranded, you have to do your best by her. She may be saved by your efforts, by your resource and fortitude bearing up against the heavy weight of guilt and failure. And there are justifiable strandings in fogs, on uncharted seas, on dangerous shores, through treacherous tides. But, saved or not saved, there remains with her commander a distinct sense of loss, a flavor in the mouth of the real, abiding danger that lurks in all the forms of human existence. It is an acquisition, too, that feeling. A man may be the better for it, but he will not be the same. Damocles has seen the sword suspended by a hair over his head, and though a good man need not be made less valuable by such a knowledge, the feast shall not henceforth have the same flavor.

Years ago I was concerned as chief mate in a case of stranding which was not fatal to the ship. We went to work for ten hours on end, laying out anchors in readiness to heave off at high water. While I was still busy about the decks forward I heard the steward at my elbow saying: "The captain asks whether you mean to come in, sir, and have something to eat today."

I went into the cuddy. My captain sat at the head of the table like a statue. There was a strange motionlessness of everything in that pretty little cabin. The swing-table which for seventy odd days had been always on the move, if ever so little, hung quite still above the soup-tureen. Nothing could have altered the rich color of my commander's complexion, laid on generously by wind and sea; but between the two tufts of fair hair above his ears, his skull, generally suffused with the hue of blood, shone dead white, like a dome of ivory. And he looked strangely untidy. I perceived he had not shaved himself that day; and yet the wildest motion of the ship in the most stormy latitudes we had passed through, never made him miss one single morning ever since we left the Channel. The fact must be that a commander cannot possibly shave himself when his ship is aground. I have commanded ships myself, but I don't know; I have never tried to shave in my life.

He did not offer to help me or himself till I had coughed markedly several times. I talked to him professionally in a cheery tone, and ended with the confident assertion:

"We shall get her off before midnight, sir."

He smiled faintly without looking up, and muttered as if to himself:

"Yes, yes; the captain put the ship ashore and we got her off."

Then, raising his head, he attacked grumpily the steward, a lanky, anxious youth with a long, pale face and two big front teeth.

"What makes this soup so bitter? I am surprised the mate can swallow the beastly stuff. I'm sure the cook's ladled some salt water into it by mistake."

The charge was so outrageous that the steward for all answer only dropped his eyelids bashfully.

There was nothing the matter with the soup. I had

a second helping. My heart was warm with hours of hard work at the head of a willing crew. I was elated with having handled heavy anchors, cables, boats without the slightest hitch; pleased with having laid out scientifically bower, stream, and kedge exactly where I believed they would do most good. On that occasion the bitter taste of a stranding was not for my mouth. That experience came later, and it was only then that I understood the loneliness of the man in charge.

It's the captain who puts the ship ashore; it's we who get her off.

Chapter XXII

*I*t seems to me that no man born and truthful to himself could declare that he ever saw the sea looking young as the earth looks young in spring. But some of us, regarding the ocean with understanding and affection, have seen it looking old, as if the immemorial ages had been stirred up from the undisturbed bottom of ooze. For it is a gale of wind that makes the sea look old.

From a distance of years, looking at the remembered aspects of the storms lived through, it is that impression which disengages itself clearly from the great body of impressions left by many years of intimate contact.

If you would know the age of the earth, look upon the sea in a storm. The grayness of the whole immense surface, the wind furrows upon the faces of the waves, the great masses of foam, tossed about and waving, like matted white locks, give to the sea in a gale an appearance of hoary age, lusterless, dull, without gleams, as though it had been created before light itself.

Looking back after much love and much trouble, the instinct of primitive man, who seeks to personify the forces of Nature for his affection and for his fear, is awakened again in the breast of one civilized beyond that stage even in his infancy. One seems to have known gales as enemies, and even as enemies one embraces them in that affectionate regret which clings to the past.

Gales have their personalities, and, after all, perhaps it is not strange; for, when all is said and done, they are adversaries whose wiles you must defeat, whose violence you must resist, and yet with whom you must live in the intimacies of nights and days.

Here speaks the man of masts and sails, to whom the sea is not a navigable element, but an intimate companion. The length of passages, the growing sense of solitude, the close dependence upon the very forces that, friendly today, without changing their nature, by the mere putting forth of their might, become dangerous tomorrow, make for that sense of fellowship which modern seamen, good men as they are, cannot hope to know. And, besides, your modern ship which is a steamship makes her passages on other principles than yielding to the weather and humoring the sea. She receives smashing blows, but she advances; it is a slogging fight, and not a scientific campaign. The machinery, the steel, the fire, the steam, have stepped in between the man and the sea. A modern fleet of ships does not so much make use of the sea as exploit a highway. The modern ship is not the sport of the waves. Let us say that each of her voyages is a triumphant progress; and yet it is a question whether it is not a more subtle and more human triumph to be the sport of the waves and yet survive, achieving your end.

In his own time a man is always very modern. Whether the seamen of three hundred years hence will have the faculty of sympathy it is impossible to say. An incorrigible mankind hardens its heart in the progress of its own perfectibility. How will they feel on seeing the illustrations to the sea novels of our day, or of our yesterday? It is impossible to guess. But the seaman of the last generation, brought into sympathy with the caravels of ancient time by his sailing-ship, their lineal descendant, cannot look upon those lumbering forms navigating the naïve seas of ancient woodcuts without a feeling of surprise, of affectionate derision, envy, and admiration. For those things, whose unmanageableness, even when represented on paper, makes one gasp with a sort of amused horror, were manned by men who are his direct professional ancestors.

No; the seamen of three hundred years hence will probably be neither touched nor moved to derision, affection, or admiration. They will glance at the photogravures of our nearly defunct sailing-ships with a cold, inquisitive and indifferent eye. Our ships of yesterday will stand to their ships as no lineal ancestors, but as mere predecessors whose course will have been run and the race extinct. Whatever craft he handles with skill, the seaman of the future shall be, not our descendant, but only our successor.

Chapter XXIII

*A*nd so much depends upon the craft which, made by man, is one with man, that the sea shall wear for him another aspect. I remember once seeing the commander — officially the master, by courtesy the captain — of a fine iron ship of the old wool fleet shaking his head at a very pretty brigantine. She was bound the other way. She was a taut, trim, neat little craft, extremely well kept; and on that serene evening when we passed her close she looked the embodiment of coquettish comfort on the sea. It was somewhere near the Cape — *the* Cape being, of course, the Cape of Good Hope, the Cape of Storms of its Portuguese discoverer. And whether it is that the word "storm" should not be pronounced upon the sea where the storms dwell thickly, or because men are shy of confessing their good hopes, it has become the nameless cape — the Cape *tout court*. The other great cape of the world, strangely enough, is seldom if ever called a cape. We say, "a voyage round the Horn"; "we rounded the Horn"; "we got a frightful battering off the Horn"; but rarely "Cape Horn," and, indeed, with some reason, for Cape Horn is as much an island as a cape. The third stormy cape of the world, which is the Leeuwin, receives generally its full name, as if to console its second-rate dignity. These are the capes that look upon the gales.

The little brigantine, then, had doubled the Cape. Perhaps she was coming from Port Elizabeth, from East London — who knows? It was many years ago, but I remember well the captain of the wool-clipper nodding at her with the words, "Fancy having to go about the sea in a thing like that!"

He was a man brought up in big deep-water ships, and the size of the craft under his feet was a part of his conception of the sea. His own ship was certainly big as ships went then. He may have thought of the size of his cabin, or — unconsciously, perhaps — have conjured up a vision of a vessel so small tossing amongst the great seas. I didn't inquire, and to a young second mate the captain of the little pretty brigantine, sitting astride a camp stool with his chin resting on his hands that were crossed upon the rail, might have appeared a minor king amongst men. We passed her within earshot, without a hail, reading each other's names with the naked eye.

Some years later, the second mate, the recipient of that almost involuntary mutter, could have told his captain that a man brought up in big ships may yet take a peculiar delight in what we should both then have called a small craft. Probably the captain of the big ship would not have understood very well. His answer would have been a gruff, "Give me size," as I heard another man reply to a remark praising the handiness of a small vessel. It was not a love of the grandiose or the prestige attached to the command of great tonnage, for he continued, with an air of disgust and contempt, "Why, you get flung out of your bunk as likely as not in any sort of heavy weather."

I don't know. I remember a few nights in my life-time, and in a big ship, too (as big as they made them then), when one did not get flung out of one's bed simply because one never even attempted to get in; one had been made too weary, too hopeless, to try. The expedient of turning your bedding out on to a damp floor and lying on it there was no earthly good, since you could not keep your place or get a second's rest in that or any other position. But of the delight of seeing a small craft run bravely amongst the great seas there can be no question to him whose soul does not dwell ashore. Thus I well remember a three days' run got out of a little barque of 400 tons somewhere between the islands of St. Paul and Amsterdam and Cape Otway on the Australian coast. It was a hard, long gale, gray clouds and green sea, heavy weather undoubtedly, but still what a sailor would call manageable. Under two lower topsails and a reefed foresail the barque seemed to race with a long, steady sea that did not becalm her in the troughs. The solemn thundering combers caught her up from astern, passed her with a fierce boiling up of foam level with the bulwarks, swept on ahead with a swish and a roar: and the little vessel, dipping her jib-boom into the tumbling froth, would go on running in a smooth, glassy hollow, a deep valley between two ridges of the sea, hiding the horizon ahead and astern. There was such fascination in her pluck, nimbleness, the continual exhibition of unfailing sea-worthiness, in the semblance of courage and endur-ance, that I could not give up the delight of watching her run through the three unforgettable days of that gale which my mate also delighted to extol as "a famous shove."

And this is one of those gales whose memory in after-years returns, welcome in dignified austerity, as you would remember with pleasure the noble features of a stranger with whom you crossed swords once in knightly encounter and are never to see again. In this way gales have their physiognomy. You remember them by your own feelings, and no two gales stamp themselves in the same way upon your emotions. Some cling to you in woebegone misery; others come back fiercely and weirdly, like ghouls bent upon sucking your strength away; others, again, have a catastrophic splendor; some are unvenerated recollections, as of spiteful wildcats clawing at your agonized vitals; others are severe, like a visitation; and one or two rise up draped and mysterious, with an aspect of ominous menace. In each of them there is a characteristic point at which the whole feeling seems contained in one single moment. Thus there is a certain four o'clock in the morning in the confused roar of a black and white world when coming on deck to take charge of my watch I received the instantaneous impression that the ship could not live for another hour in such a raging sea.

I wonder what became of the men who silently (you couldn't hear yourself speak) must have shared that conviction with me. To be left to write about it is not, perhaps, the most enviable fate; but the point is that this impression resumes in its intensity the whole recollection of days and days of desperately dangerous weather. We were then, for reasons which it is not worth while to specify, in the close neighborhood of Kerguelen Land; and now, when I open an atlas and look at the tiny dots on the map of the Southern Ocean, I see as if engraved upon the paper the enraged physiognomy of that gale.

Another, strangely, recalls a silent man. And yet it was not din that was wanting; in fact, it was terrific. That one was a gale that came upon the ship swiftly, like a parnpero, which last is a very sudden wind indeed. Before we knew very well what was coming all the sails we had set had burst; the furled ones were blowing loose, ropes flying, sea hissing — it hissed tremendously — wind howling, and the ship lying on her side, so that half of the crew were swimming and the other half clawing desperately at whatever came to hand, according to the side of the deck each man had been caught on by the catastrophe, either to leeward or to windward. The shouting I need not mention — it was the merest drop in an ocean of noise — and yet the character of the gale seems contained in the recollection of one small, not particularly impressive, sallow man without a cap and with a very still face. Captain Jones — let us call him Jones — had been caught unawares. Two orders he had given at the first sign of an utterly unforeseen onset; after that the magnitude of his mistake seemed to have overwhelmed him. We were doing what was needed and feasible. The ship behaved well. Of course, it was some time before we could pause in our fierce and laborious exertions; but all through the work, the excitement, the uproar, and some dismay, we were aware of this silent little man at the break of the poop, perfectly motionless, soundless, and often hidden from us by the drift of sprays.

When we officers clambered at last upon the poop, he seemed to come out of that numbed composure, and shouted to us down wind: "Try the pumps." Afterwards he disappeared. As to the ship, I need not say that, although she was presently swallowed up in one of the blackest nights I can remember, she did not disappear. In truth, I don't fancy that there had ever been much danger of that, but certainly the experience was noisy and particularly distracting — and yet it is the memory of a very quiet silence that survives.

Chapter XXIV

*F*or, after all, a gale of wind, the thing of mighty sound, is inarticulate. It is man who, in a chance phrase, interprets the elemental passion of his enemy. Thus there is another gale in my memory, a thing of endless, deep, humming roar, moonlight, and a spoken sentence.

It was off that other cape which is always deprived of its title as the Cape of Good Hope is robbed of its name. It was off the Horn. For a true expression of disheveled wildness there is nothing like a gale in the bright moonlight of a high latitude.

The ship, brought-to and bowing to enormous flashing seas, glistened wet from deck to trucks; her one set sail stood out a coal-black shape upon the gloomy blueness of the air. I was a youngster then, and suffering from weariness, cold, and imperfect oilskins which let water in at every seam. I craved human companionship, and, coming off the poop, took my place by the side of the boatswain (a man whom I did not like) in a comparatively dry spot where at worst we had water only up to our knees. Above our heads the explosive booming gusts of wind passed continuously, justifying the sailor's saying "It blows great guns." And just from that need of human companionship, being very close to the man, I said, or rather shouted:

"Blows very hard, boatswain."

His answer was:

"Aye, and if it blows only a little harder things will begin to go. I don't mind as long as everything holds, but when things begin to go it's bad."

The note of dread in the shouting voice, the practical truth of these words, heard years ago from a man I did not like, have stamped its peculiar character on that gale.

A look in the eyes of a shipmate, a low murmur in the most sheltered spot where the watch on duty are huddled together, a meaning moan from one to the other with a glance at the windward sky, a sigh of weariness, a gesture of disgust passing into the keeping of the great wind, become part and parcel of the gale. The olive hue of hurricane clouds presents an aspect peculiarly appalling. The inky ragged wrack, flying before a nor'-west wind, makes you dizzy with its headlong speed that depicts the rush of the invisible air. A hard sou'-wester startles you with its close horizon and its low gray sky, as if the world were a dungeon wherein there is no rest for body or soul. And there are black squalls, white squalls, thunder squalls, and unexpected gusts that come without a single sign in the sky; and of each kind no one of them resembles another.

There is infinite variety in the gales of wind at sea, and except for the peculiar, terrible, and mysterious moaning that may be heard sometimes passing through the roar of a hurricane — except for that unforgettable sound, as if the soul of the universe had been goaded into a mournful groan — it is, after all, the human voice that stamps the mark of human consciousness upon the character of a gale.

Chapter XXV

*T*here is no part of the world of coasts, continents, oceans, seas, straits, capes, and islands which is not under the sway of a reigning wind, the sovereign of its typical weather. The wind rules the aspects of the sky and the action of the sea. But no wind rules unchallenged his realm of land and water. As with the kingdoms of the earth, there are regions more turbulent than others. In the middle belt of the earth the Trade Winds reign supreme, undisputed, like monarchs of long-settled kingdoms, whose traditional power, checking all undue ambitions, is not so much an exercise of personal might as the working of long-established institutions. The intertropical kingdoms of the Trade Winds are favorable to the ordinary life of a merchantman. The trumpet-call of strife is seldom borne on their wings to the watchful ears of men on the decks of ships. The regions ruled by the northeast and southeast Trade Winds are serene. In a southern-going ship, bound out for a long voyage, the passage through their dominions is characterized by a relaxation of strain and vigilance on the part of the seamen. Those citizens of the ocean feel sheltered under the aegis of an uncontested law, of an undisputed dynasty. There, indeed, if anywhere on earth, the weather may be trusted.

Yet not too implicitly. Even in the constitutional realm of Trade Winds, north and south of the equator, ships are overtaken by strange disturbances. Still, the easterly winds, and, generally speaking, the easterly weather all the world over, is characterized by regularity and persistence.

As a ruler, the East Wind has a remarkable stability; as an invader of the high latitudes lying under the tumultuous sway of his great brother, the Wind of the West, he is extremely difficult to dislodge, by the reason of his cold craftiness and profound duplicity.

The narrow seas around these isles, where British admirals keep watch and ward upon the marches of the Atlantic Ocean, are subject to the turbulent sway of the West Wind. Call it northwest or southwest, it is all one — a different phase of the same character, a changed expression on the same face. In the orientation of the winds that rule the seas, the north and south directions are of no importance. There are no North and South Winds of any account upon this earth. The North and South Winds are but small princes in the dynasties that make peace and war upon the sea. They never assert themselves upon a vast stage. They depend upon local causes — the configuration of coasts, the shapes of straits, the accidents of bold promontories round which they play their little part. In the polity of winds, as amongst the tribes of the earth, the real struggle lies between East and West.

Chapter XXVI

The West Wind reigns over the seas surrounding the coasts of these kingdoms; and from the gateways of the channels, from promontories as if from watchtowers, from estuaries of rivers as if from postern gates, from passage-ways, inlets, straits, firths, the garrison of the Isle and the crews of the ships going and returning look to the westward to judge by the varied splendors of his sunset mantle the mood of that arbitrary ruler. The end of the day is the time to gaze at the kingly face of the Westerly Weather, who is the arbiter of ships' destinies. Benignant and splendid, or splendid and sinister, the western sky reflects the hidden purposes of the royal mind. Clothed in a mantle of dazzling gold or draped in rags of black clouds like a beggar, the might of the Westerly Wind sits enthroned upon the western horizon with the whole North Atlantic as a footstool for his feet and the first twinkling stars making a diadem for his brow. Then the seamen, attentive courtiers of the weather, think of regulating the conduct of their ships by the mood of the master. The West Wind is too great a king to be a dissembler: he is no calculator plotting deep schemes in a somber heart; he is too strong for small artifices; there is passion in all his moods, even in the soft mood of his serene days, in the grace of his blue sky whose immense and unfathomable tenderness reflected in the mirror of the sea embraces, possesses, lulls to sleep the ships with white sails. He is all things to all oceans; he is like a poet seated upon a throne — magnificent, simple, barbarous, pensive, generous, impulsive, changeable, unfathomable — but when you understand him, always the same. Some of his sunsets are like pageants devised for the delight of the multitude, when all the gems of the royal treasure-house are displayed above the sea. Others are like the opening of his royal confidence, tinged with thoughts of sadness and compassion in a melancholy splendor meditating upon the short-lived peace of the waters. And I have seen him put the pent-up anger of his heart into the aspect of the inaccessible sun, and cause it to glare fiercely like the eye of an implacable autocrat out of a pale and frightened sky.

He is the war-lord who sends his battalions of Atlantic rollers to the assault of our seaboard. The compelling voice of the West Wind musters up to his service all the might of the ocean. At the bidding of the West Wind there arises a great commotion in the sky above these Islands, and a great rush of waters falls upon our shores. The sky of the westerly weather is full of flying clouds, of great big white clouds coming thicker and thicker till they seem to stand welded into a solid canopy, upon whose gray face the lower wrack of the gale, thin, black and angry-looking, flies past with vertiginous speed. Denser and denser grows this dome of vapors, descending lower and lower upon the sea, narrowing the horizon around the ship. And the characteristic aspect of westerly weather, the thick, gray, smoky and sinister tone sets in, circumscribing the view of the men, drenching their bodies, oppressing their souls, taking their breath away with booming gusts, deafening, blinding, driving, rushing them onwards in a swaying ship towards our coasts lost in mists and rain.

The caprice of the winds, like the willfulness of men, is fraught with the disastrous consequences of self-indulgence. Long anger, the sense of his uncontrolled power, spoils the frank and generous nature of the West Wind. It is as if his heart were corrupted by a malevolent and brooding rancor. He devastates his own kingdom in the wantonness of his force. Southwest is the quarter of the heavens where he presents his darkened brow. He breathes his rage in terrific squalls, and overwhelms his realm with an inexhaustible welter of clouds. He strews the seeds of anxiety upon the decks of scudding ships, makes the foam-stripped ocean look old, and sprinkles with gray hairs the heads of shipmasters in the homeward-bound ships running for the Channel. The Westerly Wind asserting his sway from the southwest quarter is often like a monarch gone mad, driving forth with wild imprecations the most faithful of his courtiers to shipwreck, disaster, and death.

The southwesterly weather is the thick weather *par excellence.* It is not the thickness of the fog; it is rather a contraction of the horizon, a mysterious veiling of the shores with clouds that seem to make a low-vaulted dungeon around the running ship. It is not blindness; it is a shortening of the sight. The West Wind does not say to the seaman, "You shall be blind"; it restricts merely the range of his vision and raises the dread of land within his breast. It makes of him a man robbed of half his force, of half his efficiency. Many times in my life, standing in long sea-boots and streaming oilskins at the elbow of my commander on the poop of a homeward-bound ship making for the Channel, and gazing ahead into the gray and tormented waste, I have heard a weary sigh shape itself into a studiously casual comment:

"Can't see very far in this weather."

And have made answer in the same low, perfunctory tone

"No, sir."

It would be merely the instinctive voicing of an ever-present thought associated closely with the consciousness of the land somewhere ahead and of the great speed of the ship. Fair wind, fair wind! Who would dare to grumble at a fair wind? It was a favor of the Western King, who rules masterfully the North Atlantic from the latitude of the Azores to the latitude of Cape Farewell. A famous shove this to end a good passage with; and yet, somehow, one could not muster upon one's lips the smile of a courtier's gratitude. This favor was dispensed to you from under an overbearing scowl, which is the true expression of the great autocrat when he has made up his mind to give a battering to some ships and to hunt certain others home in one breath of cruelty and benevolence, equally distracting.

"No, sir. Can't see very far."

Thus would the mate's voice repeat the thought of the master, both gazing ahead, while under their feet the ship rushes at some twelve knots in the direction of the lee shore; and only a couple of miles in front of her swinging and dripping jib-boom, carried naked with an upward slant like a spear, a gray horizon closes the view with a multitude of waves surging upwards violently as if to strike at the stooping clouds.

Awful and threatening scowls darken the face of the West Wind in his clouded, southwest mood; and from the King's throne-hall in the western board stronger gusts reach you, like the fierce shouts of raving fury to which only the gloomy grandeur of the scene imparts a saving dignity. A shower pelts the deck and the sails of the ship as if flung with a scream by an angry hand; and when the night closes in, the night of a southwesterly gale, it seems more hopeless than the shade of Hades. The southwesterly mood of the great West Wind is a lightless mood, without sun, moon, or stars, with no gleam of light but the phosphorescent flashes of the great sheets of foam that, boiling up on each side of the ship, fling bluish gleams upon her dark and narrow hull, rolling as she runs, chased by enormous seas, distracted in the tumult.

There are some bad nights in the kingdom of the West Wind for homeward-bound ships making for the Channel; and the days of wrath dawn upon them colorless and vague like the timid turning up of invisible lights upon the scene of a tyrannical and passionate outbreak, awful in the monotony of its method and the increasing strength of its violence. It is the same wind, the same clouds, the same wildly racing seas, the same thick horizon around the ship. Only the wind is stronger, the clouds seem denser and more overwhelming, the waves appear to have grown bigger and more threatening during the night. The hours, whose minutes are marked by the crash of the breaking seas, slip by with the screaming, pelting squalls overtaking the ship as she runs on and on with darkened canvas, with streaming spars and dripping ropes. The down-pours thicken. Preceding each shower a mysterious gloom, like the passage of a shadow above the firmament of gray clouds, filters down upon the ship. Now and then the rain pours upon your head in streams as if from spouts. It seems as if your ship were going to be drowned before she sank, as if all atmosphere had turned to water. You gasp, you splutter, you are blinded and deafened, you are submerged, obliterated, dissolved, annihilated, streaming all over as if your limbs,

too, had turned to water. And every nerve on the alert
you watch for the clearing-up mood of the Western
King, that shall come with a shift of wind as likely as
not to whip all the three masts out of your ship in the
twinkling of an eye.

Chapter XXVII

*H*eralded by the increasing fierceness of the squalls, sometimes by a faint flash of lightning like the signal of a lighted torch waved far away behind the clouds, the shift of wind comes at last, the crucial moment of the change from the brooding and veiled violence of the southwest gale to the sparkling, flashing, cutting, clear-eyed anger of the King's northwesterly mood. You behold another phase of his passion, a fury bejeweled with stars, mayhap bearing the crescent of the moon on its brow, shaking the last vestiges of its torn cloud-mantle in inky-black squalls, with hail and sleet descending like showers of crystals and pearls, bounding off the spars, drumming on the sails, pattering on the oilskin coats, whitening the decks of homeward-bound ships. Faint, ruddy flashes of lightning flicker in the starlight upon her mastheads. A chilly blast hums in the taut rigging, causing the ship to tremble to her very keel, and the soaked men on her decks to shiver in their wet clothes to the very marrow of their bones. Before one squall has flown over to sink in the eastern board, the edge of another peeps up already above the western horizon, racing up swift, shapeless, like a black bag full of frozen water ready to burst over your devoted head. The temper of the ruler of the ocean has changed. Each gust of the clouded mood that seemed warmed by the heat of a heart flaming with anger has its counterpart in the chilly blasts that seem blown from a breast turned to ice with a sudden revulsion of feeling. Instead of blinding your eyes and crushing your soul with a terrible apparatus of cloud and mists and seas and rain, the King of the West turns his power to contemptuous pelting of your back with icicles, to making your weary eyes water as if in grief, and your worn-out carcass quake pitifully. But each mood of the great autocrat has its own greatness, and each is hard to bear. Only the northwest phase of that mighty display is not demoralizing to the same extent, because between the hail and sleet squalls of a northwesterly gale one can see a long way ahead.

To see! to see! — this is the craving of the sailor, as of the rest of blind humanity. To have his path made clear for him is the aspiration of every human being in our beclouded and tempestuous existence. I have heard a reserved, silent man, with no nerves to speak of, after three days of hard running in thick south-westerly weather, burst out passionately: "I wish to God we could get sight of something!"

We had just gone down below for a moment to commune in a battened-down cabin, with a large white chart lying limp and damp upon a cold and clammy table under the light of a smoky lamp. Sprawling over that seaman's silent and trusted adviser, with one elbow upon the coast of Africa and the other planted in the neighborhood of Cape Hatteras (it was a general track-chart of the North Atlantic), my skipper lifted his rugged, hairy face, and glared at me in a half-exasper-ated, half-appealing way. We have seen no sun, moon, or stars for something like seven days. By the effect of the West Wind's wrath the celestial bodies had gone into hiding for a week or more, and the last three days had seen the force of a southwest gale grow from fresh, through strong, to heavy, as the entries in my log-book could testify. Then we separated, he to go on deck again, in obedience to that mysterious call that seems to sound forever in a shipmaster's ears, I to stagger into my cabin with some vague notion of putting down the words "Very heavy weather" in a log-book not quite written up-to-date. But I gave it up, and crawled into my bunk instead, boots and hat on, all standing (it did not matter; everything was soaking wet, a heavy sea having burst the poop skylights the night before), to remain in a nightmarish state between waking and sleeping for a couple of hours of so-called rest.

The southwesterly mood of the West Wind is an enemy of sleep, and even of a recumbent position, in the responsible officers of a ship. After two hours of futile, lightheaded, inconsequent thinking upon all things under heaven in that dark, dank, wet and devastated cabin, I arose suddenly and staggered up on deck. The autocrat of the North Atlantic was still oppressing his kingdom and its outlying dependencies, even as far as the Bay of Biscay, in the dismal secrecy of thick, very thick, weather. The force of the wind, though we were running before it at the rate of some ten knots an hour, was so great that it drove me with a steady push to the front of the poop, where my commander was holding on.

"What do you think of it?" he addressed me in an interrogative yell.

What I really thought was that we both had had just about enough of it. The manner in which the great West Wind chooses at times to administer his possessions does not commend itself to a person of peaceful and law-abiding disposition, inclined to draw distinctions between right and wrong in the face of natural forces, whose standard, naturally, is that of might alone. But, of course, I said nothing. For a man caught, as it were, between his skipper and the great West Wind silence is the safest sort of diplomacy. Moreover, I knew my skipper. He did not want to know what I thought. Shipmasters hanging on a breath before the thrones of the winds ruling the seas have their psychology, whose workings are as important to the ship and those on board of her as the changing moods of the weather. The man, as a matter of fact, under no circumstances, ever cared a brass farthing for what I or anybody else in his ship thought. He had had just about enough of it, I guessed, and what he was at really was a process of fishing for a suggestion. It was the pride of his life that he had never wasted a chance, no matter how boisterous, threatening, and dangerous, of a fair wind. Like men racing blindfold for a gap in a hedge, we were finishing a splendidly quick passage from the Antipodes, with a tremendous rush for the Channel in as thick a weather as any I can remember, but his psychology did not permit him to bring the ship to with a fair wind blowing — at least not on his own initiative. And yet he felt that very soon indeed something would have to be done. He wanted the suggestion to come from me, so that later on, when the trouble was over, he could argue this point with his own uncompromising spirit, laying the blame upon my shoulders. I must render him the justice that this sort of pride was his only weakness.

But he got no suggestion from me. I understood his psychology. Besides, I had my own stock of weaknesses at the time (it is a different one now), and amongst them was the conceit of being remarkably well up in the psychology of the Westerly weather. I believed — not to mince matters — that I had a genius for reading the mind of the great ruler of high latitudes. I fancied I could discern already the coming of a change in his royal mood. And all I said was:

"The weather's bound to clear up with the shift of wind."

"Anybody knows that much!" he snapped at me, at the highest pitch of his voice.

"I mean before dark!" I cried.

This was all the opening he ever got from me. The eagerness with which he seized upon it gave me the measure of the anxiety he had been laboring under.

"Very well," he shouted, with an affectation of impatience, as if giving way to long entreaties. "All right. If we don't get a shift by then we'll take that foresail off her and put her head under her wing for the night."

I was struck by the picturesque character of the phrase as applied to a ship brought-to in order to ride out a gale with wave after wave passing under her breast. I could see her resting in the tumult of the elements like a sea-bird sleeping in wild weather upon the raging waters with its head tucked under its wing. In imaginative precision, in true feeling, this is one of the most expressive sentences I have ever heard on human lips. But as to taking the foresail off that ship before we put her head under her wing, I had my grave doubts. They were justified. That long enduring piece of canvas was confiscated by the arbitrary decree of the West Wind, to whom belong the lives of men and the contrivances of their hands within the limits of his kingdom. With the sound of a faint explosion it vanished into the thick weather bodily, leaving behind of its stout substance not so much as one solitary strip big enough to be picked into a handful of lint for, say, a wounded elephant. Torn out of its bolt-ropes, it faded like a whiff of smoke in the smoky drift of clouds shattered and torn by the shift of wind. For the shift of wind had come. The unveiled, low sun glared angrily from a chaotic sky upon a confused and tremendous sea dashing itself upon a coast. We recognized the headland, and looked at each other in the silence of dumb wonder. Without knowing it in the least, we had run up alongside the Isle of Wight, and that tower, tinged a faint evening red in the salt wind-haze, was the lighthouse on St. Catherine's Point.

My skipper recovered first from his astonishment. His bulging eyes sank back gradually into their orbits. His psychology, taking it all round, was really very creditable for an average sailor. He had been spared the humiliation of laying his ship to with a fair wind; and at once that man, of an open and truthful nature, spoke up in perfect good faith, rubbing together his brown, hairy hands — the hands of a master-craftsman upon the sea:

"Humph! that's just about where I reckoned we had got to."

The transparency and ingenuousness, in a way, of that delusion, the airy tone, the hint of already growing pride, were perfectly delicious. But, in truth, this was one of the greatest surprises ever sprung by the clearing up mood of the West Wind upon one of the most accomplished of his courtiers.

Chapter XXVIII

The winds of North and South are, as I have said, but small princes amongst the powers of the sea. They have no territory of their own; they are not reigning winds anywhere. Yet it is from their houses that the reigning dynasties which have shared between them the waters of the earth are sprung. All the weather of the world is based upon the contest of the Polar and Equatorial strains of that tyrannous race. The West Wind is the greatest king. The East rules between the Tropics. They have shared each ocean between them. Each has his genius of supreme rule. The King of the West never intrudes upon the recognized dominion of his kingly brother. He is a barbarian, of a northern type. Violent without craftiness, and furious without malice, one may imagine him seated masterfully with a double-edged sword on his knees upon the painted and gilt clouds of the sunset, bowing his shock head of golden locks, a flaming beard over his breast, imposing, colossal, mighty-limbed, with a thundering voice, distended cheeks and fierce blue eyes, urging the speed of his gales. The other, the East king, the king of blood-red sunrises, I represent to myself as a spare

Southerner with clear-cut features, black-browed and dark-eyed, gray-robed, upright in sunshine, resting a smooth-shaven cheek in the palm of his hand, impenetrable, secret, full of wiles, fine-drawn, keen — meditating aggressions.

The West Wind keeps faith with his brother, the King of the Easterly weather. "What we have divided we have divided," he seems to say in his gruff voice, this ruler without guile, who hurls as if in sport enormous masses of cloud across the sky, and flings the great waves of the Atlantic clear across from the shores of the New World upon the hoary headlands of Old Europe, which harbors more kings and rulers upon its seamed and furrowed body than all the oceans of the world together. "What we have divided we have divided; and if no rest and peace in this world have fallen to my share, leave me alone. Let me play at quoits with cyclonic gales, flinging the discs of spinning cloud and whirling air from one end of my dismal kingdom to the other: over the Great Banks or along the edges of pack-ice — this one with true aim right into the bight of the Bay of Biscay, that other upon the fiords of Norway, across the North Sea where the fishermen of many nations look watchfully into my angry eye. This is the time of kingly sport."

And the royal master of high latitudes sighs mightily, with the sinking sun upon his breast and the double-edged sword upon his knees, as if wearied by the innumerable centuries of a strenuous rule and saddened by the unchangeable aspect of the ocean under his feet — by the endless vista of future ages where the work of sowing the wind and reaping the whirlwind shall go on and on till his realm of living waters becomes a frozen and motionless ocean. But the other, crafty and unmoved, nursing his shaven chin between the thumb and forefinger of his slim and treacherous hand, thinks deep within his heart full of guile: "Aha! our brother of the West has fallen into the mood of kingly melancholy. He is tired of playing with circular gales, and blowing great guns, and unrolling thick streamers of fog in wanton sport at the cost of his own poor, miserable subjects. Their fate is most pitiful. Let us make a foray upon the dominions of that noisy barbarian, a great raid from Finisterre to Hatteras, catching his fishermen unawares, baffling the fleets that trust to his power, and shooting sly arrows into the livers of men who court his good graces. He is, indeed, a worthless fellow." And forthwith, while the West Wind meditates upon the vanity of his irresistible might, the thing is done, and the Easterly weather sets in upon the North Atlantic.

The prevailing weather of the North Atlantic is typical of the way in which the West Wind rules his realm on which the sun never sets. North Atlantic is the heart of a great empire. It is the part of the West Wind's dominions most thickly populated with generations of fine ships and hardy men. Heroic deeds and adventurous exploits have been performed there, within the very stronghold of his sway. The best sailors in the world have been born and bred under the shadow of his scepter, learning to manage their ships with skill and audacity before the steps of his stormy throne. Reckless adventurers, toiling fishermen, admirals as wise and brave as the world has ever known, have waited upon the signs of his westerly sky. Fleets of victorious ships have hung upon his breath. He has tossed in his hand squadrons of war-scarred three-deckers, and shredded out in mere sport the bunting of flags hallowed in the traditions of honor and glory. He is a good friend and a dangerous enemy, without mercy to unseaworthy ships and faint-hearted seamen. In his kingly way he has taken but little account of lives sacrificed to his impulsive policy; he is a king with a double-edged sword bared in his right hand. The East Wind, an interloper in the dominions of Westerly weather, is an impassive-faced tyrant with a sharp poniard held behind his back for a treacherous stab.

In his forays into the North Atlantic the East Wind behaves like a subtle and cruel adventurer without a notion of honor or fair play. Veiling his clear-cut, lean face in a thin layer of a hard, high cloud, I have seen him, like a wizened robber sheik of the sea, hold up large caravans of ships to the number of three hundred or more at the very gates of the English Channel. And the worst of it was that there was no ransom that we could pay to satisfy his avidity; for whatever evil is wrought by the raiding East Wind, it is done only to spite his kingly brother of the West. We gazed helplessly at the systematic, cold, gray-eyed obstinacy of the Easterly weather, while short rations became the order of the day, and the pinch of hunger under the breast-bone grew familiar to every sailor in that held-up fleet. Every day added to our numbers. In knots and groups and straggling parties we flung to and fro before the closed gate. And meantime the outward-bound ships passed, running through our humiliated ranks under all the canvas they could show. It is my idea that the Easterly Wind helps the ships away from home in the wicked hope that they shall all come to an untimely end and be heard of no more. For six weeks did the robber sheik hold the trade route of the earth, while our liege lord, the West Wind, slept profoundly like a tired Titan, or else remained lost in a mood of idle sadness known only to frank natures. All was still to the westward; we looked in vain towards his stronghold: the King slumbered on so deeply that he let his foraging brother steal the very mantle of gold-lined purple clouds from his bowed shoulders. What had become of the dazzling hoard of royal jewels exhibited at every close of day? Gone, disappeared, extinguished, carried off without leaving a single gold band or the flash of a single sunbeam in the evening sky! Day after day through a cold streak of heavens as bare and poor as the inside of a rifled safe a rayless and despoiled sun would slink shamefacedly, without pomp or show, to hide in haste under the waters. And still the King slept on, or mourned the vanity of his might and his power, while the thin-lipped intruder put the impress of his cold and implacable spirit upon the sky and sea. With every daybreak the rising sun had to wade through a crimson stream, luminous and sinister, like the spilt blood of celestial bodies murdered during the night.

In this particular instance the mean interloper held the road for some six weeks on end, establishing his particular administrative methods over the best part of the North Atlantic. It looked as if the easterly weather had come to stay forever, or, at least, till we had all starved to death in the held-up fleet — starved within sight, as it were, of plenty, within touch, almost, of the bountiful heart of the Empire. There we were, dotting with our white dry sails the hard blueness of the deep sea. There we were, a growing company of ships, each with her burden of grain, of timber, of wool, of hides, and even of oranges, for we had one or two belated fruit schooners in company. There we were, in that memorable spring of a certain year in the late seventies, dodging to and fro, baffled on every tack, and with our stores running down to sweepings of bread-lockers and scrapings of sugar-casks. It was just like the East Wind's nature to inflict starvation upon the bodies of unoffending sailors, while he corrupted their simple souls by an exasperation leading to out-bursts of profanity as lurid as his blood-red sunrises. They were followed by gray days under the cover of high, motionless clouds that looked as if carved in a slab of ash-colored marble. And each mean starved sunset left us calling with imprecations upon the West Wind even in its most veiled misty mood to wake up and give us our liberty, if only to rush on and dash the heads of our ships against the very walls of our unapproachable home.

Chapter XXIX

*I*n the atmosphere of the Easterly weather, as pellucid as a piece of crystal and refracting like a prism, we could see the appalling numbers of our helpless company, even to those who in more normal conditions would have remained invisible, sails down under the horizon. It is the malicious pleasure of the East Wind to augment the power of your eyesight, in order, perhaps, that you should see better the perfect humiliation, the hopeless character of your captivity. Easterly weather is generally clear, and that is all that can be said for it — almost supernaturally clear when it likes; but whatever its mood, there is something uncanny in its nature. Its duplicity is such that it will deceive a scientific instrument. No barometer will give warning of an easterly gale, were it ever so wet. It would be an unjust and ungrateful thing to say that a barometer is a stupid contrivance. It is simply that the wiles of the East Wind are too much for its fundamental honesty. After years and years of experience the most trusty instrument of the sort that ever went to sea screwed on to a ship's cabin bulkhead will, almost invariably, be induced to rise by the diabolic ingenuity of the Easterly weather, just at the moment when the Easterly weather, discarding its methods of hard, dry, impassive cruelty, contemplates drowning what is left of your spirit in torrents of a peculiarly cold and horrid rain. The sleet-and-hail squalls following the lightning at the end of a westerly gale are cold and benumbing and stinging and cruel enough. But the dry, Easterly weather, when it turns to wet, seems to rain poisoned showers upon your head. It is a sort of steady, persistent, overwhelming, endlessly driving downpour, which makes your heart sick, and opens it to dismal forebodings. And the stormy mood of the Easterly weather looms black upon the sky with a peculiar and amazing blackness. The West Wind hangs heavy gray curtains of mist and spray before your gaze, but the Eastern interloper of the narrow seas, when he has mustered his courage and cruelty to the point of a gale, puts your eyes out, puts them out completely, makes you feel blind for life upon a lee-shore. It is the wind, also, that brings snow.

Out of his black and merciless heart he flings a white blinding sheet upon the ships of the sea. He has more manners of villainy, and no more conscience than an Italian prince of the seventeenth century. His weapon is a dagger carried under a black cloak when he goes out on his unlawful enterprises. The mere hint of his approach fills with dread every craft that swims the sea, from fishing-smacks to four-masted ships that recognize the sway of the West Wind. Even in his most accommodating mood he inspires a dread of treachery. I have heard upwards of ten score of windlasses spring like one into clanking life in the dead of night, filling the Downs with a panic-struck sound of anchors being torn hurriedly out of the ground at the first breath of his approach. Fortunately, his heart often fails him: he does not always blow home upon our exposed coast; he has not the fearless temper of his Westerly brother.

The natures of those two winds that share the dominions of the great oceans are fundamentally different. It is strange that the winds which men are prone to style capricious remain true to their character in all the various regions of the earth. To us here, for instance, the East Wind comes across a great continent, sweeping over the greatest body of solid land upon this earth. For the Australian east coast the East Wind is the wind of the ocean, coming across the greatest body of water upon the globe; and yet here and there its characteristics remain the same with a strange consistency in everything that is vile and base. The members of the West Wind's dynasty are modified in a way by the regions they rule, as a Hohenzollern, without ceasing to be himself, becomes a Romanian by virtue of his throne, or a Saxe-Coburg learns to put the dress of Bulgarian phrases upon his particular thoughts, whatever they are.

The autocratic sway of the West Wind, whether forty north or forty south of the Equator, is characterized by an open, generous, frank, barbarous recklessness. For he is a great autocrat, and to be a great autocrat you must be a great barbarian. I have been too much molded to his sway to nurse now any idea of rebellion in my heart. Moreover, what is a rebellion within the four walls of a room against the tempestuous rule of the West Wind? I remain faithful to the memory of the mighty King with a double-edged sword in one hand, and in the other holding out rewards of great daily runs and famously quick passages to those of his courtiers who knew how to wait watchfully for every sign of his secret mood. As we deep-water men always reckoned, he made one year in three fairly lively for anybody having business upon the Atlantic or down there along the "forties" of the Southern Ocean. You had to take the bitter with the sweet; and it cannot be denied he played carelessly with our lives and fortunes. But, then, he was always a great king, fit to rule over the great waters where, strictly speaking, a man would have no business whatever but for his audacity.

The audacious should not complain. A mere trader ought not to grumble at the tolls levied by a mighty king. His mightiness was sometimes very overwhelming; but even when you had to defy him openly, as on the banks of the Agulhas homeward bound from the East Indies, or on the outward passage round the Horn, he struck at you fairly his stinging blows (full in the face, too), and it was your business not to get too much staggered. And, after all, if you showed anything of a countenance, the good-natured barbarian would let you fight your way past the very steps of his throne. It was only now and then that the sword descended and a head fell; but if you fell you were sure of impressive obsequies and of a roomy, generous grave.

Such is the king to whom Viking chieftains bowed their heads, and whom the modern and palatial steamship defies with impunity seven times a week. And yet it is but defiance, not victory. The magnificent barbarian sits enthroned in a mantle of gold-lined clouds looking from on high on great ships gliding like mechanical toys upon his sea and on men who, armed with fire and iron, no longer need to watch anxiously for the slightest sign of his royal mood. He is disregarded; but he has kept all his strength, all his splendor, and a great part of his power. Time itself, that shakes all the thrones, is on the side of that king. The sword in his hand remains as sharp as ever upon both its edges; and he may well go on playing his royal game of quoits with hurricanes, tossing them over from the continent of republics to the continent of kingdoms, in the assurance that both the new republics and the old kingdoms, the heat of fire and the strength of iron, with the untold generations of audacious men, shall crumble to dust at the steps of his throne, and pass away, and be forgotten before his own rule comes to an end.

Chapter XXX

*T*he estuaries of rivers appeal strongly to an adventurous imagination. This appeal is not always a charm, for there are estuaries of a particularly dispiriting ugliness: lowlands, mud-flats, or perhaps barren sand hills without beauty of form or amenity of aspect, covered with a shabby and scanty vegetation conveying the impression of poverty and uselessness. Sometimes such an ugliness is merely a repulsive mask. A river whose estuary resembles a breach in a sand rampart may flow through a most fertile country. But all the estuaries of great rivers have their fascination, the attractiveness of an open portal. Water is friendly to man. The ocean, a part of Nature furthest removed in the unchangeableness and majesty of its might from the spirit of mankind, has ever been a friend to the enterprising nations of the earth. And of all the elements this is the one to which men have always been prone to trust themselves, as if its immensity held a reward as vast as itself.

From the offing the open estuary promises every possible fruition to adventurous hopes. That road open to enterprise and courage invites the explorer of coasts to new efforts towards the fulfillment of great expectations. The commander of the first Roman galley must have looked with an intense absorption upon the estuary of the Thames as he turned the beaked prow of his ship to the westward under the brow of the North Foreland. The estuary of the Thames is not beautiful; it has no noble features, no romantic grandeur of aspect, no smiling geniality; but it is wide open, spacious, inviting, hospitable at the first glance, with a strange air of mysteriousness which lingers about it to this very day. The navigation of his craft must have engrossed all the Roman's attention in the calm of a summer's day (he would choose his weather), when the single row of long sweeps (the galley would be a light one, not a trireme) could fall in easy cadence upon a sheet of water like plate-glass, reflecting faithfully the classic form of his vessel and the contour of the lonely shores close on his left hand. I assume he followed the land and passed through what is at present known as Margate Roads, groping his careful way along the hidden sandbanks, whose every tail and spit has its beacon or buoy nowadays. He must have been anxious, though no doubt he had collected beforehand on the shores of the Gauls a store of information from the talk of traders, adventurers, fishermen, slave-dealers, pirates — all sorts of unofficial men connected with the sea in a more or less reputable way. He would have heard of channels and sandbanks, of natural features of the land useful for sea-marks, of villages and tribes and modes of barter and precautions to take: with the instructive tales about native chiefs dyed more or less blue, whose character for greediness, ferocity, or amiability must have been expounded to him with that capacity for vivid language which seems joined naturally to the shadiness of moral character and recklessness of disposition. With that sort of spiced food provided for his anxious thought, watchful for strange men, strange beasts, strange turns of the tide, he would make the best of his way up, a military seaman with a short sword on thigh and a bronze helmet on his head, the pioneer post-captain of an imperial fleet. Was the tribe inhabiting the Isle of Thanet of a ferocious disposition, I wonder, and ready to fall with stone-studded clubs and wooden lances hardened in the fire, upon the backs of unwary mariners?

Amongst the great commercial streams of these islands, the Thames is the only one, I think, open to romantic feeling, from the fact that the sight of human labor and the sounds of human industry do not come down its shores to the very sea, destroying the suggestion of mysterious vastness caused by the configuration of the shore. The broad inlet of the shallow North Sea passes gradually into the contracted shape of the river; but for a long time the feeling of the open water remains with the ship steering to the westward through one of the lighted and buoyed passage-ways of the Thames, such as Queen's Channel, Prince's Channel, Four-Fathom Channel; or else coming down the Swin from the north. The rush of the yellow flood-tide hurries her up as if into the unknown between the two fading lines of the coast. There are no features to this land, no conspicuous, far-famed landmarks for the eye; there is nothing so far down to tell you of the greatest agglomeration of mankind on earth dwelling no more than five and twenty miles away, where the sun sets in a blaze of color flaming on a gold background, and the dark, low shores trend towards each other. And in the great silence the deep, faint booming of the big guns being tested at Shoeburyness hangs about the Nore — a historical spot in the keeping of one of England's appointed guardians.

Chapter XXXI

*T*he Nore sand remains covered at low-water, and never seen by human eye; but the Nore is a name to conjure with visions of historical events, of battles, of fleets, of mutinies, of watch and ward kept upon the great throbbing heart of the State. This ideal point of the estuary, this center of memories, is marked upon the steely gray expanse of the waters by a lightship painted red that, from a couple of miles off, looks like a cheap and bizarre little toy. I remember how, on coming up the river for the first time, I was surprised at the smallness of that vivid object — a tiny warm speck of crimson lost in an immensity of gray tones. I was startled, as if of necessity the principal beacon in the water-way of the greatest town on earth should have presented imposing proportions. And, behold! the brown sprit-sail of a barge hid it entirely from my view.

Coming in from the eastward, the bright coloring of the lightship marking the part of the river committed to the charge of an Admiral (the Commander-in-Chief at the Nore) accentuates the dreariness and the great breadth of the Thames Estuary. But soon the course of the ship opens the entrance of the Medway, with its men-of-war moored in line, and the long wooden jetty of Port Victoria, with its few low buildings like the beginning of a hasty settlement upon a wild and unexplored shore. The famous Thames barges sit in brown clusters upon the water with an effect of birds floating upon a pond. On the imposing expanse of the great estuary the traffic of the port where so much of the world's work and the world's thinking is being done becomes insignificant, scattered, streaming away in thin lines of ships stringing themselves out into the eastern quarter through the various navigable channels of which the Nore lightship marks the divergence. The coasting traffic inclines to the north; the deep-water ships steer east with a southern inclination, on through the Downs, to the most remote ends of the world. In the widening of the shores sinking low in the gray, smoky distances the greatness of the sea receives the mercantile fleet of good ships that London sends out upon the turn of every tide. They follow each other, going very close by the Essex shore. Such as the beads of a rosary told by businesslike ship owners for the greater profit of the world they slip one by one into the open: while in the offing the inward-bound ships come up singly and in bunches from under the sea horizon closing the mouth of the river between Orfordness and North Foreland. They all converge upon the Nore, the warm speck of red upon the tones of drab and gray, with the distant shores running together towards the west, low and flat, like the sides of an enormous canal. The sea-reach of the Thames is straight, and, once Sheerness is left behind, its banks seem very uninhabited, except for the cluster of houses which is Southend, or here and there a lonely wooden jetty where petroleum ships discharge their dangerous cargoes, and the oil-storage tanks, low and round with slightly-domed roofs, peep over the edge of the foreshore, as it were a village of Central African huts imitated in iron. Bordered by the black and shining mud-flats, the level marsh extends for miles. Away in the far background the land rises, closing the view with a continuous wooded slope, forming in the distance an interminable rampart overgrown with bushes.

Then, on the slight turn of the Lower Hope Reach, clusters of factory chimneys come distinctly into view, tall and slender above the squat ranges of cement works in Grays and Greenhithe. Smoking quietly at the top against the great blaze of a magnificent sunset, they give an industrial character to the scene, speak of work, manufactures, and trade, as palm-groves on the coral strands of distant islands speak of the luxuriant grace, beauty and vigor of tropical nature. The houses of Gravesend crowd upon the shore with an effect of confusion as if they had tumbled down haphazard from the top of the hill at the back. The flatness of the Kentish shore ends there. A fleet of steam-tugs lies at anchor in front of the various piers. A conspicuous church spire, the first seen distinctly coming from the sea, has a thoughtful grace, the serenity of a fine form above the chaotic disorder of men's houses. But on the other side, on the flat Essex side, a shapeless and desolate red edifice, a vast pile of bricks with many windows and a slate roof more inaccessible than an Alpine slope, towers over the bend in monstrous ugliness, the tallest, heaviest building for miles around, a thing like an hotel, like a mansion of flats (all to let), exiled into these fields out of a street in West Kensington. Just round the corner, as it were, on a pier defined with stone blocks and wooden piles, a white mast, slender like a stalk of straw and crossed by a yard like a knitting-needle, flying the signals of flag and balloon, watches over a set of heavy dock-gates. Mast-heads and funnel-tops of ships peep above the ranges of corrugated iron roofs. This is the entrance to Tilbury Dock, the most recent of all London docks, the nearest to the sea.

Between the crowded houses of Gravesend and the monstrous red-brick pile on the Essex shore the ship is surrendered fairly to the grasp of the river. That hint of loneliness, that soul of the sea which had accompanied her as far as the Lower Hope Reach, abandons her at the turn of the first bend above. The salt, acrid flavor is gone out of the air, together with a sense of unlimited space opening free beyond the threshold of sandbanks below the Nore. The waters of the sea rush on past Gravesend, tumbling the big mooring buoys laid along the face of the town; but the sea-freedom stops short there, surrendering the salt tide to the needs, the artifices, the contrivances of toiling men. Wharves, landing-places, dock-gates, waterside stairs, follow each other continuously right up to London Bridge, and the hum of men's work fills the river with a menacing, muttering note as of a breathless, ever-driving gale. The water-way, so fair above and wide below, flows oppressed by bricks and mortar and stone, by blackened timber and grimed glass and rusty iron, covered with black barges, whipped up by paddles and screws, overburdened with craft, overhung with chains, overshadowed by walls making a steep gorge for its bed, filled with a haze of smoke and dust.

This stretch of the Thames from London Bridge to the Albert Docks is to other watersides of river ports what a virgin forest would be to a garden. It is a thing grown up, not made. It recalls a jungle by the confused, varied, and impenetrable aspect of the buildings that line the shore, not according to a planned purpose, but as if sprung up by accident from scattered seeds. Like the matted growth of bushes and creepers veiling the silent depths of an unexplored wilderness, they hide the depths of London's infinitely varied, vigorous, seething life. In other river ports it is not so. They lie open to their stream, with quays like broad clearings, with streets like avenues cut through thick timber for the convenience of trade. I am thinking now of river ports I have seen — of Antwerp, for instance; of Nantes or Bordeaux, or even old Rouen, where the night-watchmen of ships, elbows on rail, gaze at shop windows and brilliant cafés, and see the audience go in and come out of the opera-house. But London, the oldest and greatest of river ports, does not possess as much as a hundred yards of open quays upon its riverfront. Dark and impenetrable at night, like the face of a forest, is the London waterside. It is the waterside of watersides, where only one aspect of the world's life can be seen, and only one kind of men toils on the edge of the stream. The lightless walls seem to spring from the very mud upon which the stranded barges lie; and the narrow lanes coming down to the foreshore resemble the paths of smashed bushes and crumbled earth where big game comes to drink on the banks of tropical streams.

Behind the growth of the London waterside the docks of London spread out unsuspected, smooth, and placid, lost amongst the buildings like dark lagoons hidden in a thick forest. They lie concealed in the intricate growth of houses with a few stalks of mast-heads here and there overtopping the roof of some four-story warehouse.

It is a strange conjunction this of roofs and mast-heads, of walls and yard-arms. I remember once having the incongruity of the relation brought home to me in a practical way. I was the chief officer of a fine ship, just docked with a cargo of wool from Sydney, after a ninety days' passage. In fact, we had not been in more than half an hour and I was still busy making her fast

to the stone posts of a very narrow quay in front of a
lofty warehouse. An old man with a gray whisker under
the chin and brass buttons on his pilot-cloth jacket,
hurried up along the quay hailing my ship by name.
He was one of those officials called berthing-masters
— not the one who had berthed us, but another, who,
apparently, had been busy securing a steamer at the
other end of the dock. I could see from afar his hard
blue eyes staring at us, as if fascinated, with a queer
sort of absorption. I wondered what that worthy sea-
dog had found to criticize in my ship's rigging. And
I, too, glanced aloft anxiously. I could see nothing
wrong there. But perhaps that superannuated fellow-
craftsman was simply admiring the ship's perfect order
aloft, I thought, with some secret pride; for the chief
officer is responsible for his ship's appearance, and as
to her outward condition, he is the man open to praise
or blame. Meantime the old salt ("ex-coasting skipper"
was writ large all over his person) had hobbled up
alongside in his bumpy, shiny boots, and, waving an
arm, short and thick like the flipper of a seal, termi-
nated by a paw red as an uncooked beef-steak, addressed the poop in a muffled, faint, roaring voice, as
if a sample of every North-Sea fog of his life had been
permanently lodged in his throat: "Haul 'em round,
Mr. Mate!" were his words. "If you don't look sharp,
you'll have your topgallant yards through the windows
of that 'ere warehouse presently!" This was the only
cause of his interest in the ship's beautiful spars. I own
that for a time I was struck dumb by the bizarre
associations of yard-arms and windowpanes. To break
windows is the last thing one would think of in con-
nection with a ship's topgallant yard, unless, indeed,
one were an experienced berthing-master in one of the
London docks. This old chap was doing his little share
of the world's work with proper efficiency. His little

blue eyes had made out the danger many hundred yards off. His rheumaticky feet, tired with balancing that squat body for many years upon the decks of small coasters, and made sore by miles of tramping upon the flagstones of the dock side, had hurried up in time to avert a ridiculous catastrophe. I answered him pettishly, I fear, and as if I had known all about it before.

"All right, all right! can't do everything at once."

He remained near by, muttering to himself till the yards had been hauled round at my order, and then raised again his foggy, thick voice:

"None too soon," he observed, with a critical glance up at the towering side of the warehouse. "That's a half-sovereign in your pocket, Mr. Mate. You should always look first how you are for them windows before you begin to breast in your ship to the quay."

It was good advice. But one cannot think of everything or foresee contacts of things apparently as remote as stars and hop-poles.

Chapter XXXII

The view of ships lying moored in some of the older docks of London has always suggested to my mind the image of a flock of swans kept in the flooded backyard of grim tenement houses. The flatness of the walls surrounding the dark pool on which they float brings out wonderfully the flowing grace of the lines on which a ship's hull is built. The lightness of these forms, devised to meet the winds and the seas, makes, by contrast with the great piles of bricks, the chains and cables of their moorings appear very necessary, as if nothing less could prevent them from soaring upwards and over the roofs. The least puff of wind stealing round the corners of the dock buildings stirs these captives fettered to rigid shores. It is as if the soul of a ship were impatient of confinement. Those masted hulls, relieved of their cargo, become restless at the slightest hint of the wind's freedom. However tightly moored, they range a little at their berths, swaying imperceptibly the spirelike assemblages of cordage and spars. You can detect their impatience by watching the sway of the mastheads against the motionless, the soulless gravity of mortar and stones. As you pass alongside each hopeless prisoner chained to the quay, the slight grinding noise of the wooden fenders makes a sound of angry muttering. But, after all, it may be good for ships to go through a period of restraint and repose, as the restraint and self-communion of inactivity may be good for an unruly soul — not, indeed, that I mean to say that ships are unruly; on the contrary, they are faithful creatures, as so many men can testify. And faithfulness is a great restraint, the strongest bond laid upon the self-will of men and ships on this globe of land and sea.

This interval of bondage in the docks rounds each period of a ship's life with the sense of accomplished duty, of an effectively played part in the work of the world. The dock is the scene of what the world would think the most serious part in the light, bounding, swaying life of a ship. But there are docks and docks. The ugliness of some docks is appalling. Wild horses would not drag from me the name of a certain river in the north whose narrow estuary is inhospitable and dangerous, and whose docks are like a nightmare of dreariness and misery. Their dismal shores are studded thickly with scaffoldlike, enormous timber structures, whose lofty heads are veiled periodically by the infernal gritty night of a cloud of coal-dust. The most important ingredient for getting the world's work along is distributed there under the circumstances of the greatest cruelty meted out to helpless ships. Shut up in the desolate circuit of these basins, you would think a free ship would droop and die like a wild bird put into a dirty cage. But a ship, perhaps because of her faithfulness to men, will endure an extraordinary lot of ill-usage. Still, I have seen ships issue from certain docks like half-dead prisoners from a dungeon, bedraggled, overcome, wholly disguised in dirt, and with their men rolling white eyeballs in black and worried faces raised to a heaven which, in its smoky and soiled aspect, seemed to reflect the sordidness of the earth below. One thing, however, may be said for the docks of the Port of London on both sides of the river: for all the complaints of their insufficient equipment, of their obsolete rules, of failure (they say) in the matter of quick dispatch, no ship need ever issue from their gates in a half-fainting condition. London is a general cargo port, as is only proper for the greatest capital of the world to be. General cargo ports belong to the aristocracy of the earth's trading places, and in that aristocracy London, as it is its way, has a unique physiognomy.

The absence of picturesqueness cannot be laid to the charge of the docks opening into the Thames. For all my unkind comparisons to swans and backyards, it cannot be denied that each dock or group of docks along the north side of the river has its own individual attractiveness. Beginning with the cozy little St. Katherine's Dock, lying overshadowed and black like a quiet pool amongst rocky crags, through the venerable and sympathetic London Docks, with not a single line of rails in the whole of their area and the aroma of spices lingering between its warehouses, with their far-famed wine-cellars — down through the interesting group of West India Docks, the fine docks at Blackwall, on past the Galleons Reach entrance of the Victoria and Albert Docks, right down to the vast gloom of the great basins in Tilbury, each of those places of restraint for ships has its own peculiar physiognomy, its own expression. And what makes them unique and attractive is their common trait of being romantic in their usefulness.

In their way they are as romantic as the river they serve is unlike all the other commercial streams of the world. The coziness of the St. Katherine's Dock, the old-world air of the London Docks, remain impressed upon the memory. The docks down the river, abreast of Woolwich, are imposing by their proportions and the vast scale of the ugliness that forms their surroundings — ugliness so picturesque as to become a delight to the eye. When one talks of the Thames docks, "beauty" is a vain word, but romance has lived too long upon this river not to have thrown a mantle of glamour upon its banks.

The antiquity of the port appeals to the imagination by the long chain of adventurous enterprises that had their inception in the town and floated out into the world on the waters of the river. Even the newest of the docks, the Tilbury Dock, shares in the glamour conferred by historical associations. Queen Elizabeth has made one of her progresses down there, not one of her journeys of pomp and ceremony, but an anxious business progress at a crisis of national history. The menace of that time has passed away, and now Tilbury is known by its docks. These are very modern, but their remoteness and isolation upon the Essex marsh, the days of failure attending their creation, invested them with a romantic air. Nothing in those days could have been more striking than the vast, empty basins, surrounded by miles of bare quays and the ranges of cargo-sheds, where two or three ships seemed lost like bewitched children in a forest of gaunt, hydraulic cranes. One received a wonderful impression of utter abandonment, of wasted efficiency. From the first the Tilbury Docks were very efficient and ready for their task, but they had come, perhaps, too soon into the field. A great future lies before Tilbury Docks. They shall never fill a long-felt want (in the sacramental phrase that is applied to railways, tunnels, newspapers, and new editions of books). They were too early in the field. The want shall never be felt because, free of the trammels of the tide, easy of access, magnificent and desolate, they are already there, prepared to take and keep the biggest ships that float upon the sea. They are worthy of the oldest river port in the world.

And, truth to say, for all the criticisms flung upon the heads of the dock companies, the other docks of the Thames are no disgrace to the town with a population greater than that of some commonwealths. The growth of London as a well-equipped port has been slow, while not unworthy of a great capital, of a great center of distribution. It must not be forgotten that London has not the backing of great industrial districts or great fields of natural exploitation. In this it differs from Liverpool, from Cardiff, from Newcastle, from Glasgow; and therein the Thames differs from the Mersey, from the Tyne, from the Clyde. It is an historical river; it is a romantic stream flowing through the center of great affairs, and for all the criticism of the river's administration, my contention is that its development has been worthy of its dignity. For a long time the stream itself could accommodate quite easily the oversea and coasting traffic. That was in the days when, in the part called the Pool, just below London Bridge, the vessels moored stem and stern in the very strength of the tide formed one solid mass like an island covered with a forest of gaunt, leafless trees; and when the trade had grown too big for the river there came the St. Katherine's Docks and the London Docks, magnificent undertakings answering to the need of their time. The same may be said of the other artificial lakes full of ships that go in and out upon this high road to all parts of the world. The labor of the imperial waterway goes on from generation to generation, goes on day and night. Nothing ever arrests its sleepless industry but the coming of a heavy fog, which clothes the teeming stream in a mantle of impenetrable stillness.

After the gradual cessation of all sound and movement on the faithful river, only the ringing of ships' bells is heard, mysterious and muffled in the white vapor from London Bridge right down to the Nore, for miles and miles in a decrescendo tinkling, to where the estuary broadens out into the North Sea, and the anchored ships lie scattered thinly in the shrouded channels between the sandbanks of the Thames' mouth. Through the long and glorious tale of years of the river's strenuous service to its people these are its only breathing times.

Chapter XXXIII

A ship in dock, surrounded by quays and the walls
of warehouses, has the appearance of a prisoner meditating upon freedom in the sadness of a free spirit put
under restraint. Chain cables and stout ropes keep her
bound to stone posts at the edge of a paved shore, and
a berthing-master, with brass buttons on his coat, walks
about like a weather-beaten and ruddy jailer, casting
jealous, watchful glances upon the moorings that fetter
a ship lying passive and still and safe, as if lost in deep
regrets of her days of liberty and danger on the sea.

The swarm of renegades — dock-masters, berthing-
masters, gatemen, and such like — appear to nurse an
immense distrust of the captive ship's resignation.
There never seem chains and ropes enough to satisfy
their minds concerned with the safe binding of free
ships to the strong, muddy, enslaved earth. "You had
better put another bight of a hawser astern, Mr. Mate,"
is the usual phrase in their mouth. I brand them for
renegades, because most of them have been sailors in
their time. As if the infirmities of old age — the gray
hair, the wrinkles at the corners of the eyes, and the
knotted veins of the hands — were the symptoms of

moral poison, they prowl about the quays with an underhand air of gloating over the broken spirit of noble captives. They want more fenders, more breasting-ropes; they want more springs, more shackles, more fetters; they want to make ships with volatile souls as motionless as square blocks of stone. They stand on the mud of pavements, these degraded sea-dogs, with long lines of railway-trucks clanking their couplings behind their backs, and run malevolent glances over your ship from headgear to taffrail, only wishing to tyrannize over the poor creature under the hypocritical cloak of benevolence and care. Here and there cargo cranes looking like instruments of torture for ships swing cruel hooks at the end of long chains. Gangs of dock-laborers swarm with muddy feet over the gangways. It is a moving sight this, of so many men of the earth, earthy, who never cared anything for a ship, trampling unconcerned, brutal and hob-nailed upon her helpless body.

Fortunately, nothing can deface the beauty of a ship. That sense of a dungeon, that sense of a horrible and degrading misfortune overtaking a creature fair to see and safe to trust, attaches only to ships moored in the docks of great European ports. You feel that they are dishonestly locked up, to be hunted about from wharf to wharf on a dark, greasy, square pool of black water as a brutal reward at the end of a faithful voyage.

A ship anchored in an open roadstead, with cargo-lighters alongside and her own tackle swinging the burden over the rail, is accomplishing in freedom a function of her life. There is no restraint; there is space: clear water around her, and a clear sky above her mastheads, with a landscape of green hills and charming bays opening around her anchorage. She is not abandoned by her own men to the tender mercies of shore people. She still shelters, and is looked after by, her own little devoted band, and you feel that presently she will glide between the headlands and disappear. It is only at home, in dock, that she lies abandoned, shut off from freedom by all the artifices of men that think of quick dispatch and profitable freights. It is only then that the odious, rectangular shadows of walls and roofs fall upon her decks, with showers of soot.

To a man who has never seen the extraordinary nobility, strength, and grace that the devoted generations of ship-builders have evolved from some pure nooks of their simple souls, the sight that could be seen five-and-twenty years ago of a large fleet of clippers moored along the north side of the New South Dock was an inspiring spectacle. Then there was a quarter of a mile of them, from the iron dockyard-gates guarded by policemen, in a long, forestlike perspective of masts, moored two and two to many stout wooden jetties. Their spars dwarfed with their loftiness the corrugated-iron sheds, their jibbooms extended far over the shore, their white-and-gold figure-heads, almost dazzling in their purity, overhung the straight, long quay above the mud and dirt of the wharfside, with the busy figures of groups and single men moving to and fro, restless and grimy under their soaring immobility.

At tide-time you would see one of the loaded ships with battened-down hatches drop out of the ranks and float in the clear space of the dock, held by lines dark and slender, like the first threads of a spider's web, extending from her bows and her quarters to the mooring-posts on shore. There, graceful and still, like a bird ready to spread its wings, she waited till, at the opening of the gates, a tug or two would hurry in noisily, hovering round her with an air of fuss and solicitude, and take her out into the river, tending, shepherding her through open bridges, through damlike gates between the flat pier-heads, with a bit of green lawn surrounded by gravel and a white signal-mast with yard and gaff, flying a couple of dingy blue, red, or white flags.

This New South Dock (it was its official name), round which my earlier professional memories are centered, belongs to the group of West India Docks, together with two smaller and much older basins called Import and Export respectively, both with the greatness of their trade departed from them already. Picturesque and clean as docks go, these twin basins spread side by side the dark luster of their glassy water, sparely peopled by a few ships laid up on buoys or tucked far away from each other at the end of sheds in the corners of empty quays, where they seemed to slumber quietly remote, untouched by the bustle of men's affairs — in retreat rather than in captivity. They were quaint and sympathetic, those two homely basins, unfurnished and silent, with no aggressive display of cranes, no apparatus of hurry and work on their narrow shores. No railway-lines cumbered them. The knots of laborers trooping in clumsily round the corners of cargo-sheds to eat their food in peace out of red cotton handkerchiefs had the air of picnicking by the side of a lonely mountain pool. They were restful (and I should say very unprofitable), those basins, where the chief officer of one of the ships involved in the harassing, strenuous, noisy activity of the New South Dock only a few yards away could escape in the dinner-hour to stroll, unhampered by men and affairs, meditating (if he chose) on the vanity of all things human. At one time they must have been full of good old slow West Indiamen of the square-stern type, that took their captivity, one imagines, as stolidly as they had faced the buffeting of the waves with their blunt, honest bows, and disgorged sugar, rum, molasses, coffee, or logwood sedately with their own winch and tackle. But when I knew them, of exports there was never a sign that one could detect; and all the imports I have ever seen were some rare cargoes of tropical timber, enormous baulks roughed out of iron trunks grown in the woods about the Gulf of Mexico. They lay piled up in stacks of mighty boles, and it was hard to believe that all this mass of dead and stripped trees had come out of the flanks of a slender, innocent-looking little barque with, as likely as not, a homely woman's name — Ellen this or Annie that — upon her fine bows. But this is generally the case with a discharged cargo. Once spread at large over the quay, it looks the most impossible bulk to have all come there out of that ship along-side.

They were quiet, serene nooks in the busy world of docks, these basins where it has never been my good luck to get a berth after some more or less arduous passage. But one could see at a glance that men and ships were never hustled there. They were so quiet that, remembering them well, one comes to doubt that they ever existed — places of repose for tired ships to dream in, places of meditation rather than work, where wicked ships — the cranky, the lazy, the wet, the bad sea boats, the wild steerers, the capricious, the pig-headed, the generally ungovernable — would have full leisure to take count and repent of their sins, sorrowful and naked, with their rent garments of sailcloth stripped off them, and with the dust and ashes of the London atmosphere upon their mastheads. For that the worst of ships would repent if she were ever given time I make no doubt. I have known too many of them. No ship is wholly bad; and now that their bodies that had braved so many tempests have been blown off the face of the sea by a puff of steam, the evil and the good together into the limbo of things that have served their time, there can be no harm in affirming that in these vanished generations of willing servants there never has been one utterly unredeemable soul.

In the New South Dock there was certainly no time for remorse, introspection, repentance, or any phenomena of inner life either for the captive ships or for their officers. From six in the morning till six at night the hard labor of the prison-house, which rewards the valiance of ships that win the harbor went on steadily, great slings of general cargo swinging over the rail, to drop plumb into the hatchways at the sign of the gangway-tender's hand. The New South Dock was especially a loading dock for the Colonies in those great (and last) days of smart wool-clippers, good to look at and — well — exciting to handle. Some of them were more fair to see than the others; many were (to put it mildly) somewhat overmasted; all were expected to make good passages; and of all that line of ships, whose rigging made a thick, enormous network against the sky, whose brasses flashed almost as far as the eye of the policeman at the gates could reach, there was hardly one that knew of any other port amongst all the ports on the wide earth but London and Sydney, or London and Melbourne, or London and Adelaide, perhaps with Hobart Town added for those of smaller tonnage. One could almost have believed, as her gray-whiskered second mate used to say of the old Duke of S———, that they knew the road to the Antipodes better than their own skippers, who, year in, year out, took them from London — the place of captivity — to some Australian port where, twenty-five years ago, though moored well and tight enough to the wooden wharves, they felt themselves no captives, but honored guests.

Chapter XXXIV

*T*hese towns of the Antipodes, not so great then as they are now, took an interest in the shipping, the running links with "home," whose numbers confirmed the sense of their growing importance. They made it part and parcel of their daily interests. This was especially the case in Sydney, where, from the heart of the fair city, down the vista of important streets, could be seen the wool-clippers lying at the Circular Quay — no walled prison-house of a dock that, but the integral part of one of the finest, most beautiful, vast, and safe bays the sun ever shone upon. Now great steam-liners lie at these berths, always reserved for the sea aristocracy — grand and imposing enough ships, but here today and gone next week; whereas the general cargo, emigrant, and passenger clippers of my time, rigged with heavy spars, and built on fine lines, used to remain for months together waiting for their load of wool. Their names attained the dignity of household words. On Sundays and holidays the citizens trooped down, on visiting bent, and the lonely officer on duty solaced himself by playing the cicerone — especially to the citizenesses with engaging manners and a well-developed sense of the fun that may be got out of the inspection of a ship's cabins and state-rooms. The tinkle of more or less untuned cottage pianos floated out of open stern-ports till the gas-lamps began to twinkle in the streets, and the ship's night-watchman, coming sleepily on duty after his unsatisfactory day slumbers, hauled down the flags and fastened a lighted lantern at the break of the gangway. The night closed rapidly upon the silent ships with their crews on shore. Up a short, steep ascent by the King's Head pub., patronized by the cooks and stewards of the fleet, the voice of a man crying "Hot saveloys!" at the end of George Street, where the cheap eating-houses (sixpence a meal) were kept by Chinamen (Sun-kum-on's was not bad), is heard at regular intervals. I have listened for hours to this most pertinacious peddler (I wonder whether he is dead or has made a fortune), while sitting on the rail of the old Duke of S———(she's dead, poor thing! a violent death on the coast of New Zealand), fascinated by the monotony, the regularity, the abruptness of the recurring cry, and so exasperated at the absurd spell, that I wished the fellow would choke himself to death with a mouthful of his own infamous wares.

A stupid job, and fit only for an old man, my comrades used to tell me, to be the night-watchman of a captive (though honored) ship. And generally the oldest of the able seamen in a ship's crew does get it. But sometimes neither the oldest nor any other fairly steady seaman is forthcoming. Ships' crews had the trick of melting away swiftly in those days. So, probably on account of my youth, innocence, and pensive habits (which made me sometimes dilatory in my work about the rigging), I was suddenly nominated, in our chief mate Mr. B———'s most sardonic tones, to that enviable situation. I do not regret the experience. The night humors of the town descended from the street to the waterside in the still watches of the night: larrikins rushing down in bands to settle some quarrel by a stand-up fight, away from the police, in an indistinct ring half hidden by piles of cargo, with the sounds of blows, a groan now and then, the stamping of feet, and the cry of "Time!" rising suddenly above the sinister and excited murmurs; night-prowlers, pursued or pursuing, with a stifled shriek followed by a profound silence, or slinking stealthily along-side like ghosts, and addressing me from the quay below in mysterious tones with incomprehensible propositions. The cabmen, too, who twice a week, on the night when the A.S.N. Company's passenger-boat was due to arrive, used to range a battalion of blazing lamps opposite the ship, were very amusing in their way. They got down from their perches and told each other impolite stories in racy language, every word of which reached me distinctly over the bulwarks as I sat smoking on the main-hatch. On one occasion I had an hour or so of a most intellectual conversation with a person whom I could not see distinctly, a gentleman from England, he said, with a cultivated voice, I on deck and he on the quay sitting on the case of a piano (landed out of our hold that very afternoon), and smoking a cigar which smelt very good. We touched, in our discourse, upon science, politics, natural history, and operatic singers. Then, after remarking abruptly, "You seem to be rather intelligent, my man," he informed me pointedly that his name was Mr. Senior, and walked off — to his hotel, I suppose. Shadows! Shadows! I think I saw a white whisker as he turned under the lamp-post. It is a shock to think that in the natural course of nature he must be dead by now. There was nothing to object to in his intelligence but a little dogmatism maybe. And his name was Senior! Mr. Senior!

The position had its drawbacks, however. One wintry, blustering, dark night in July, as I stood sleepily out of the rain under the break of the poop something resembling an ostrich dashed up the gangway. I say ostrich because the creature, though it ran on two legs, appeared to help its progress by working a pair of short wings; it was a man, however, only his coat, ripped up the back and flapping in two halves above his shoulders, gave him that weird and fowllike appearance. At least, I suppose it was his coat, for it was impossible to make him out distinctly. How he managed to come so straight upon me, at speed and without a stumble over a strange deck, I cannot imagine. He must have been able to see in the dark better than any cat. He overwhelmed me with panting entreaties to let him take shelter till morning in our forecastle. Following my strict orders, I refused his request, mildly at first, in a sterner tone as he insisted with growing impudence.

"For God's sake let me, matey! Some of 'em are after me — and I've got hold of a ticker here."

"You clear out of this!" I said.

"Don't be hard on a chap, old man!" he whined pitifully.

"Now then, get ashore at once. Do you hear?"

Silence. He appeared to cringe, mute, as if words had failed him through grief; then — bang! came a concussion and a great flash of light in which he vanished, leaving me prone on my back with the most abominable black eye that anybody ever got in the faithful discharge of duty. Shadows! Shadows! I hope he escaped the enemies he was fleeing from to live and flourish to this day. But his fist was uncommonly hard and his aim miraculously true in the dark.

There were other experiences, less painful and more funny for the most part, with one amongst them of a dramatic complexion; but the greatest experience of them all was Mr. B———, our chief mate himself.

He used to go ashore every night to foregather in some hotel's parlor with his crony, the mate of the barque Cicero, lying on the other side of the Circular Quay. Late at night I would hear from afar their stumbling footsteps and their voices raised in endless argument. The mate of the Cicero was seeing his friend on board. They would continue their senseless and muddled discourse in tones of profound friendship for half an hour or so at the shore end of our gangway, and then I would hear Mr. B——— insisting that he must see the other on board his ship. And away they would go, their voices, still conversing with excessive amity, being heard moving all round the harbor. It happened more than once that they would thus per-ambulate three or four times the distance, each seeing the other on board his ship out of pure and disinter-ested affection. Then, through sheer weariness, or per-haps in a moment of forgetfulness, they would manage to part from each other somehow, and by-and-by the planks of our long gangway would bend and creak under the weight of Mr. B——— coming on board for good at last.

On the rail his burly form would stop and stand swaying.

"Watchman!"

"Sir."

A pause.

He waited for a moment of steadiness before nego-tiating the three steps of the inside ladder from rail to deck; and the watchman, taught by experience, would forbear offering help which would be received as an insult at that particular stage of the mate's return. But many times I trembled for his neck. He was a heavy man.

Then with a rush and a thump it would be done. He

never had to pick himself up; but it took him a minute or so to pull himself together after the descent.

"Watchman!"

"Sir."

"Captain aboard?"

"Yes, sir."

Pause.

"Dog aboard?"

"Yes, sir."

Pause.

Our dog was a gaunt and unpleasant beast, more like a wolf in poor health than a dog, and I never noticed Mr. B—— at any other time show the slightest interest in the doings of the animal. But that question never failed.

"Let's have your arm to steady me along."

I was always prepared for that request. He leaned on me heavily till near enough the cabin door to catch hold of the handle. Then he would let go my arm at once.

"That'll do. I can manage now."

And he could manage. He could manage to find his way into his berth, light his lamp, get into his bed — aye, and get out of it when I called him at half-past five, the first man on deck, lifting the cup of morning coffee to his lips with a steady hand, ready for duty as though he had virtuously slept ten solid hours — a better chief officer than many a man who had never tasted grog in his life. He could manage all that, but could never manage to get on in life.

Only once he failed to seize the cabin-door handle at the first grab. He waited a little, tried again, and again failed. His weight was growing heavier on my arm. He sighed slowly.

"D-n that handle!"

Without letting go his hold of me he turned about,

his face lit up bright as day by the full moon.

"I wish she were out at sea," he growled savagely.

"Yes, sir."

I felt the need to say something, because he hung on to me as if lost, breathing heavily.

"Ports are no good — ships rot, men go to the devil!"

I kept still, and after a while he repeated with a sigh.

"I wish she were at sea out of this."

"So do I, sir," I ventured.

Holding my shoulder, he turned upon me.

"You! What's that to you where she is? You don't — drink."

And even on that night he "managed it" at last. He got hold of the handle. But he did not manage to light his lamp (I don't think he even tried), though in the morning as usual he was the first on deck, bull-necked, curly-headed, watching the hands turn-to with his sardonic expression and unflinching gaze.

I met him ten years afterwards, casually, unexpectedly, in the street, on coming out of my consignee office. I was not likely to have forgotten him with his "I can manage now." He recognized me at once, remembered my name, and in what ship I had served under his orders. He looked me over from head to foot.

"What are you doing here?" he asked.

"I am commanding a little barque," I said, "loading here for Mauritius." Then, thoughtlessly, I added: "And what are you doing, Mr. B———?"

"I," he said, looking at me unflinchingly, with his old sardonic grin — "I am looking for something to do."

I felt I would rather have bitten out my tongue. His jet-black, curly hair had turned iron-gray; he was scrupulously neat as ever, but frightfully threadbare. His shiny boots were worn down at heel. But he forgave me, and we drove off together in a hansom to dine on board my ship. He went over her conscientiously, praised her heartily, congratulated me on my command with absolute sincerity. At dinner, as I offered him wine and beer he shook his head, and as I sat looking at him interrogatively, muttered in an undertone:

"I've given up all that."

After dinner we came again on deck. It seemed as though he could not tear himself away from the ship. We were fitting some new lower rigging, and he hung about, approving, suggesting, giving me advice in his old manner. Twice he addressed me as "My boy," and corrected himself quickly to "Captain." My mate was about to leave me (to get married), but I concealed the fact from Mr. B———. I was afraid he would ask me to give him the berth in some ghastly jocular hint that I could not refuse to take. I was afraid. It would have been impossible. I could not have given orders to Mr. B———, and I am sure he would not have taken them from me very long. He could not have managed that, though he had managed to break himself from drink — too late.

He said good-bye at last. As I watched his burly, bull-necked figure walk away up the street, I wondered with a sinking heart whether he had much more than the price of a night's lodging in his pocket. And I understood that if that very minute I were to call out after him, he would not even turn his head. He, too, is no more than a shadow, but I seem to hear his words spoken on the moonlit deck of the old Duke — :

"Ports are no good — ships rot, men go to the devil!"

Chapter XXXV

"Ships!" exclaimed an elderly seaman in clean shore togs. "Ships" — and his keen glance, turning away from my face, ran along the vista of magnificent figure-heads that in the late seventies used to overhang in a serried rank the muddy pavement by the side of the New South Dock — "ships are all right; it's the men in 'em . . ."

Fifty hulls, at least, molded on lines of beauty and speed — hulls of wood, of iron, expressing in their forms the highest achievement of modern ship-building — lay moored all in a row, stem to quay, as if assembled there for an exhibition, not of a great industry, but of a great art. Their colors were gray, black, dark green, with a narrow strip of yellow molding defining their sheer, or with a row of painted ports decking in warlike decoration their robust flanks of cargo-carriers that would know no triumph but of speed in carrying a burden, no glory other than of a long service, no victory but that of an endless, obscure contest with the sea. The great empty hulls with swept holds, just out of dry-dock, with their paint glistening freshly, sat high-sided with ponderous dignity alongside the wooden jetties, looking more like unmovable buildings than things meant to go afloat; others, half loaded, far on the way to recover the true sea-physiognomy of a ship brought down to her load-line, looked more accessible. Their less steeply slanting gangways seemed to invite the strolling sailors in search of a berth to walk on board and try "for a chance" with the chief mate, the guardian of a ship's efficiency. As if anxious to remain unperceived amongst their overtopping sisters, two or three "finished" ships floated low, with an air of straining at the leash of their level headfasts, exposing to view their cleared decks and covered hatches, prepared to drop stern first out of the laboring ranks, displaying the true comeliness of form which only her proper sea-trim gives to a ship. And for a good quarter of a mile, from the dockyard gate to the farthest corner, where the old housed-in hulk, the President (drill-ship, then, of the Naval Reserve), used to lie with her frigate side rubbing against the stone of the quay, above all these hulls, ready and unready, a hundred and fifty lofty masts, more or less, held out the web of their rigging like an immense net, in whose close mesh, black against the sky, the heavy yards seemed to be entangled and suspended.

It was a sight. The humblest craft that floats makes its appeal to a seaman by the faithfulness of her life; and this was the place where one beheld the aristocracy of ships. It was a noble gathering of the fairest and the swiftest, each bearing at the bow the carved emblem of her name, as in a gallery of plaster-casts, figures of women with mural crowns, women with flowing robes, with gold fillets on their hair or blue scarves round their waists, stretching out rounded arms as if to point the way; heads of men helmeted or bare; full lengths of warriors, of kings, of statesmen, of lords and princesses, all white from top to toe; with here and there a dusky turbaned figure, bedizened in many colors, of some Eastern sultan or hero, all inclined forward under the slant of mighty bowsprits as if eager to begin another run of 11,000 miles in their leaning attitudes. These were the fine figure-heads of the finest ships afloat. But why, unless for the love of the life those effigies shared with us in their wandering impassivity, should one try to reproduce in words an impression of whose fidelity there can be no critic and no judge, since such an exhibition of the art of shipbuilding and the art of figure-head carving as was seen from year's end to year's end in the open-air gallery of the New South Dock no man's eye shall behold again? All that patient, pale company of queens and princesses, of kings and warriors, of allegorical women, of heroines and statesmen and heathen gods, crowned, helmeted, bare-headed, has run for good off the sea stretching to the last above the tumbling foam their fair, rounded arms; holding out their spears, swords, shields, tridents in the same unwearied, striving forward pose. And nothing remains but lingering perhaps in the memory of a few men, the sound of their names, vanished a long time ago from the first page of the great London dailies; from big posters in railway-stations and the doors of shipping offices; from the minds of sailors, dockmasters, pilots, and tugmen; from the hail of gruff voices and the flutter of signal flags exchanged between ships closing upon each other and drawing apart in the open immensity of the sea.

The elderly, respectable seaman, withdrawing his gaze from that multitude of spars, gave me a glance to make sure of our fellowship in the craft and mystery of the sea. We had met casually, and had got into contact as I had stopped near him, my attention being caught by the same peculiarity he was looking at in the rigging of an obviously new ship, a ship with her reputation all to make yet in the talk of the seamen who were to share their life with her. Her name was already on their lips. I had heard it uttered between two thick, red-necked fellows of the semi-nautical type at the Fenchurch Street Railway-station, where, in those days, the everyday male crowd was attired in jerseys and pilot-cloth mostly, and had the air of being more conversant with the times of high-water than with the times of the trains. I had noticed that new ship's name on the first page of my morning paper. I had stared at the unfamiliar grouping of its letters, blue on white ground, on the advertisement-boards, whenever the train came to a standstill alongside one of the shabby, wooden, wharflike platforms of the dock railway-line. She had been named, with proper observances, on the day she came off the stocks, no doubt, but she was very far yet from "having a name." Untried, ignorant of the ways of the sea, she had been thrust amongst that renowned company of ships to load for her maiden voyage. There was nothing to vouch for her soundness and the worth of her character, but the reputation of the building-yard whence she was launched headlong into the world of waters. She looked modest to me. I imagined her diffident, lying very quiet, with her side nestling shyly against the wharf to which she was made fast with very new lines, intimidated by the company of her tried and experienced sisters already familiar with all the violences of the ocean and the exacting love of men. They had had more long voyages to make their names in than she had known weeks of carefully tended life, for a new ship receives as much attention as if she were a young bride. Even crabbed old dock-masters look at her with benevolent eyes. In her shyness at the threshold of a laborious and uncertain life, where so much is expected of a ship, she could not have been better heartened and comforted, had she only been able to hear and understand, than by the tone of deep conviction in which my elderly, respectable seaman repeated the first part of his saying, "Ships are all right . . ."

His civility prevented him from repeating the other, the bitter part. It had occurred to him that it was perhaps indelicate to insist. He had recognized in me a ship's officer, very possibly looking for a berth like himself, and so far a comrade, but still a man belonging to that sparsely-peopled after-end of a ship, where a great part of her reputation as a "good ship," in seaman's parlance, is made or marred.

"Can you say that of all ships without exception?" I asked, being in an idle mood, because, if an obvious ship's officer, I was not, as a matter of fact, down at the docks to "look for a berth," an occupation as engrossing as gambling, and as little favorable to the free exchange of ideas, besides being destructive of the kindly temper needed for casual intercourse with one's fellow-creatures.

"You can always put up with 'em," opined the respectable seaman judicially.

He was not averse from talking, either. If he had come down to the dock to look for a berth, he did not seem oppressed by anxiety as to his chances. He had the serenity of a man whose estimable character is fortunately expressed by his personal appearance in an unobtrusive, yet convincing, manner which no chief officer in want of hands could resist. And, true enough, I learned presently that the mate of the Hyperion had "taken down" his name for quarter-master. "We sign on Friday, and join next day for the morning tide," he remarked, in a deliberate, careless tone, which contrasted strongly with his evident readiness to stand there yarning for an hour or so with an utter stranger.

"Hyperion," I said. "I don't remember ever seeing

that ship anywhere. What sort of a name has she got?"

It appeared from his discursive answer that she had not much of a name one way or another. She was not very fast. It took no fool, though, to steer her straight, he believed. Some years ago he had seen her in Calcutta, and he remembered being told by somebody then, that on her passage up the river she had carried away both her hawse-pipes. But that might have been the pilot's fault. Just now, yarning with the apprentices on board, he had heard that this very voyage, brought up in the Downs, outward bound, she broke her sheer, struck adrift, and lost an anchor and chain. But that might have occurred through want of careful tending in a tideway. All the same, this looked as though she were pretty hard on her ground-tackle. Didn't it? She seemed a heavy ship to handle, anyway. For the rest, as she had a new captain and a new mate this voyage, he understood, one couldn't say how she would turn out. . . .

In such marine shore-talk as this is the name of a ship slowly established, her fame made for her, the tale of her qualities and of her defects kept, her idiosyncrasies commented upon with the zest of personal gossip, her achievements made much of, her faults glossed over as things that, being without remedy in our imperfect world, should not be dwelt upon too much by men who, with the help of ships, wrest out a bitter living from the rough grasp of the sea. All that talk makes up her "name," which is handed over from one crew to another without bitterness, without animosity, with the indulgence of mutual dependence, and with the feeling of close association in the exercise of her perfections and in the danger of her defects.

This feeling explains men's pride in ships. "Ships are all right," as my middle-aged, respectable quartermaster said with much conviction and some irony; but they are not exactly what men make them. They have their own nature; they can of themselves minister to our self-esteem by the demand their qualities make upon our skill and their shortcomings upon our hardiness and endurance. Which is the more flattering exaction it is hard to say; but there is the fact that in listening for upwards of twenty years to the sea-talk that goes on afloat and ashore I have never detected the true note of animosity. I won't deny that at sea, sometimes, the note of profanity was audible enough in those chiding interpellations a wet, cold, weary seaman addresses to his ship, and in moments of exasperation is disposed to extend to all ships that ever were launched — to the whole everlastingly exacting brood that swims in deep waters. And I have heard curses launched at the unstable element itself, whose fascination, outlasting the accumulated experience of ages, had captured him as it had captured the generations of his forebears.

For all that has been said of the love that certain natures (on shore) have professed to feel for it, for all the celebrations it had been the object of in prose and song, the sea has never been friendly to man. At most it has been the accomplice of human restlessness, and playing the part of dangerous abettor of world-wide ambitions. Faithful to no race after the manner of the kindly earth, receiving no impress from valor and toil and self-sacrifice, recognizing no finality of dominion, the sea has never adopted the cause of its masters like those lands where the victorious nations of mankind have taken root, rocking their cradles and setting up their gravestones. He — man or people — who, putting his trust in the friendship of the sea, neglects the strength and cunning of his right hand, is a fool! As if it were too great, too mighty for common virtues, the ocean has no compassion, no faith, no law, no memory. Its fickleness is to be held true to men's purposes only by an undaunted resolution and by a sleepless, armed, jealous vigilance, in which, perhaps, there has always been more hate than love. *Odi et amo* may well be the confession of those who consciously or blindly have surrendered their existence to the fascination of the sea. All the tempestuous passions of mankind's young days, the love of loot and the love of glory, the love of adventure and the love of danger, with the great love of the unknown and vast dreams of dominion and power, have passed like images reflected from a mirror, leaving no record upon the mysterious face of the sea. Impenetrable and heartless, the sea has given nothing of itself to the suitors for its precarious favors. Unlike the earth, it cannot be subjugated at any cost of patience and toil. For all its fascination that has lured so many to a violent death, its immensity has never been loved as the mountains, the plains, the desert itself, have been loved. Indeed, I suspect that, leaving aside the protestations and tributes of writers who, one is safe in saying, care for little else in the world than the rhythm of their lines and the cadence of their phrase, the love of the sea, to which some men and nations confess so readily, is a complex sentiment wherein pride enters for much, necessity for not a little, and the love of ships — the untiring servants of our hopes and our self-esteem — for the best and most genuine part. For the hundreds who have reviled the sea, beginning with Shakespeare in the line

"More fell than hunger, anguish, or the sea,"

down to the last obscure sea-dog of the "old model," having but few words and still fewer thoughts, there could not be found, I believe, one sailor who has ever coupled a curse with the good or bad name of a ship. If ever his profanity, provoked by the hardships of the sea, went so far as to touch his ship, it would be lightly, as a hand may, without sin, be laid in the way of kindness on a woman.

Chapter XXXVI

*T*he love that is given to ships is profoundly different from the love men feel for every other work of their hands — the love they bear to their houses, for instance — because it is untainted by the pride of possession. The pride of skill, the pride of responsibility, the pride of endurance there may be, but otherwise it is a disinterested sentiment. No seaman ever cherished a ship, even if she belonged to him, merely because of the profit she put in his pocket. No one, I think, ever did; for a ship-owner, even of the best, has always been outside the pale of that sentiment embracing in a feeling of intimate, equal fellowship the ship and the man, backing each other against the implacable, if sometimes dissembled, hostility of their world of waters. The sea — this truth must be confessed — has no generosity. No display of manly qualities — courage, hardihood, endurance, faithfulness — has ever been known to touch its irresponsible consciousness of power. The ocean has the conscienceless temper of a savage autocrat spoiled by much adulation. He cannot brook the slightest appearance of defiance, and has remained the irreconcilable enemy of ships and men ever since ships and men had the unheard of audacity to go afloat together in the face of his frown. From that day he has gone on swallowing up fleets and men without his resentment being glutted by the number of victims — by so many wrecked ships and wrecked lives. Today, as ever, he is ready to beguile and betray, to smash and to drown the incorrigible optimism of men who, backed by the fidelity of ships, are trying to wrest from him the fortune of their house, the dominion of their world, or only a dole of food for their hunger. If not always in the hot mood to smash, he is always stealthily ready for a drowning. The most amazing wonder of the deep is its unfathomable cruelty.

I felt its dread for the first time in mid-Atlantic one day, many years ago, when we took off the crew of a Danish brig homeward bound from the West Indies. A thin, silvery mist softened the calm and majestic splendor of light without shadows — seemed to render the sky less remote and the ocean less immense. It was one of the days, when the might of the sea appears indeed lovable, like the nature of a strong man in moments of quiet intimacy. At sunrise we had made out a black speck to the westward, apparently suspended high up in the void behind a stirring, shimmering veil of silvery blue gauze that seemed at times to stir and float in the breeze which fanned us slowly along. The peace of that enchanting forenoon was so profound, so untroubled, that it seemed that every word pronounced loudly on our deck would penetrate to the very heart of that infinite mystery born from the conjunction of water and sky. We did not raise our voices. "A water-logged derelict, I think, sir," said the second officer quietly, coming down from aloft with the binoculars in their case slung across his shoulders; and our captain, without a word, signed to the helmsman to steer for the black speck. Presently we made out a low, jagged stump sticking up forward — all that remained of her departed masts.

The captain was expatiating in a low conversational tone to the chief mate upon the danger of these derelicts, and upon his dread of coming upon them at night, when suddenly a man forward screamed out, "There's people on board of her, sir! I see them!" in a most extraordinary voice — a voice never heard before in our ship; the amazing voice of a stranger. It gave the signal for a sudden tumult of shouts. The watch below ran up the forecastle head in a body, the cook dashed out of the galley. Everybody saw the poor fellows now. They were there! And all at once our ship, which had the well-earned name of being without a rival for speed in light winds, seemed to us to have lost the power of motion, as if the sea, becoming viscous, had clung to her sides. And yet she moved. Immensity, the inseparable companion of a ship's life, chose that day to breathe upon her as gently as a sleeping child. The clamor of our excitement had died out, and our living ship, famous for never losing steerage way as long as there was air enough to float a feather, stole, without a ripple, silent and white as a ghost, towards her mutilated and wounded sister, come upon at the point of death in the sunlit haze of a calm day at sea.

With the binoculars glued to his eyes, the captain said in a quavering tone: "They are waving to us with something aft there." He put down the glasses on the skylight brusquely, and began to walk about the poop. "A shirt or a flag," he ejaculated irritably. "Can't make it out . . . Some damn rag or other!" He took a few more turns on the poop, glancing down over the rail now and then to see how fast we were moving. His nervous footsteps rang sharply in the quiet of the ship, where the other men, all looking the same way, had forgotten themselves in a staring immobility. "This will never do!" he cried out suddenly. "Lower the boats at once! Down with them!"

Before I jumped into mine he took me aside, as being an inexperienced junior, for a word of warning:

"You look out as you come alongside that she doesn't take you down with her. You understand?"

He murmured this confidentially, so that none of the men at the falls should overhear, and I was shocked. "Heavens! as if in such an emergency one stopped to think of danger!" I exclaimed to myself mentally, in scorn of such cold-blooded caution.

It takes many lessons to make a real seaman, and I got my rebuke at once. My experienced commander seemed in one searching glance to read my thoughts on my ingenuous face.

"What you're going for is to save life, not to drown your boat's crew for nothing," he growled severely in my ear. But as we shoved off he leaned over and cried out: "It all rests on the power of your arms, men. Give way for life!"

We made a race of it, and I would never have believed that a common boat's crew of a merchantman could keep up so much determined fierceness in the regular swing of their stroke. What our captain had clearly perceived before we left had become plain to all of us since. The issue of our enterprise hung on a hair above that abyss of waters which will not give up its dead till the Day of Judgment. It was a race of two ship's boats matched against Death for a prize of nine men's lives, and Death had a long start. We saw the crew of the brig from afar working at the pumps — still pumping on that wreck, which already had settled so far down that the gentle, low swell, over which our boats rose and fell easily without a check to their speed, welling up almost level with her head-rails, plucked at the ends of broken gear swinging desolately under her naked bow-sprit.

We could not, in all conscience, have picked out a better day for our regatta had we had the free choice of all the days that ever dawned upon the lonely struggles and solitary agonies of ships since the Norse rovers first steered to the westward against the run of Atlantic waves. It was a very good race. At the finish there was not an oar's length between the first and second boat, with Death coming in a good third on the top of the very next smooth swell, for all one knew to the contrary. The scuppers of the brig gurgled softly all together when the water rising against her sides subsided sleepily with a low wash, as if playing about an immovable rock. Her bulwarks were gone fore and aft, and one saw her bare deck low-lying like a raft and swept clean of boats, spars, houses — of everything except the ringbolts and the heads of the pumps. I had one dismal glimpse of it as I braced myself up to receive upon my breast the last man to leave her, the captain, who literally let himself fall into my arms.

It had been a weirdly silent rescue — a rescue without a hail, without a single uttered word, without a gesture or a sign, without a conscious exchange of glances. Up to the very last moment those on board stuck to their pumps, which spouted two clear streams of water upon their bare feet. Their brown skin showed through the rents of their shirts; and the two small bunches of half-naked, tattered men went on bowing from the waist to each other in their back-breaking labor, up and down, absorbed, with no time for a glance over the shoulder at the help that was coming to them. As we dashed, unregarded, alongside a voice let out one, only one hoarse howl of command, and then, just as they stood, without caps, with the salt drying gray in the wrinkles and folds of their hairy, haggard faces, blinking stupidly at us their red eyelids, they made a bolt away from the handles, tottering and jostling against each other, and positively flung themselves over upon our very heads. The clatter they made tumbling into the boats had an extraordinarily destructive effect upon the illusion of tragic dignity our self-esteem had thrown over the contests of mankind with the sea. On that exquisite day of gently breathing peace and veiled sunshine perished my romantic love to what men's imagination had proclaimed the most august aspect of Nature. The cynical indifference of the sea to the merits of human suffering and courage, laid bare in this ridiculous, panic-tainted performance extorted from the dire extremity of nine good and honorable seamen, revolted me. I saw the duplicity of the sea's most tender mood. It was so because it could not help itself, but the awed respect of the early days was gone. I felt ready to smile bitterly at its enchanting charm and glare viciously at its furies. In a moment, before we shoved off, I had looked coolly at the life of my choice. Its illusions were gone, but its fascination remained. I had become a seaman at last.

We pulled hard for a quarter of an hour, then laid on our oars waiting for our ship. She was coming down on us with swelling sails, looking delicately tall and exquisitely noble through the mist. The captain of the brig, who sat in the stern sheets by my side with his face in his hands, raised his head and began to speak with a sort of somber volubility. They had lost their masts and sprung a leak in a hurricane; drifted for weeks, always at the pumps, met more bad weather; the ships they sighted failed to make them out, the leak gained upon them slowly, and the seas had left them nothing to make a raft of. It was very hard to see ship after ship pass by at a distance, "as if everybody had agreed that we must be left to drown," he added. But they went on trying to keep the brig afloat as long as possible, and working the pumps constantly on insufficient food, mostly raw, till "yesterday evening," he continued monotonously, "just as the sun went down, the men's hearts broke."

He made an almost imperceptible pause here, and went on again with exactly the same intonation:

"They told me the brig could not be saved, and they thought they had done enough for themselves. I said nothing to that. It was true. It was no mutiny. I had nothing to say to them. They lay about aft all night, as still as so many dead men. I did not lie down. I kept a look-out. When the first light came I saw your ship at once. I waited for more light; the breeze began to fail on my face. Then I shouted out as loud as I was able, 'Look at that ship!' but only two men got up very slowly and came to me. At first only we three stood alone, for a long time, watching you coming down to us, and feeling the breeze drop to a calm almost; but afterwards others, too, rose, one after another, and by-and-by I had all my crew behind me. I turned round and said to them that they could see the ship was coming our way, but in this small breeze she might come too late after all, unless we turned to and tried to keep the brig afloat long enough to give you time to save us all. I spoke like that to them, and then I gave the command to man the pumps."

He gave the command, and gave the example, too, by going himself to the handles, but it seems that these men did actually hang back for a moment, looking at each other dubiously before they followed him. "He! he! he!" He broke out into a most unexpected, imbecile, pathetic, nervous little giggle. "Their hearts were broken so! They had been played with too long," he explained apologetically, lowering his eyes, and became silent.

Twenty-five years is a long time — a quarter of a

century is a dim and distant past; but to this day I remember the dark-brown feet, hands, and faces of two of these men whose hearts had been broken by the sea. They were lying very still on their sides on the bottom boards between the thwarts, curled up like dogs. My boat's crew, leaning over the looms of their oars, stared and listened as if at the play. The master of the brig looked up suddenly to ask me what day it was.

They had lost the date. When I told him it was Sunday, the 22nd, he frowned, making some mental calculation, then nodded twice sadly to himself, staring at nothing.

His aspect was miserably unkempt and wildly sorrowful. Had it not been for the unquenchable candor of his blue eyes, whose unhappy, tired glance every moment sought his abandoned, sinking brig, as if it could find rest nowhere else, he would have appeared mad. But he was too simple to go mad, too simple with that manly simplicity which alone can bear men unscathed in mind and body through an encounter with the deadly playfulness of the sea or with its less abominable fury.

Neither angry, nor playful, nor smiling, it enveloped our distant ship growing bigger as she neared us, our boats with the rescued men and the dismantled hull of the brig we were leaving behind, in the large and placid embrace of its quietness, half lost in the fair haze, as if in a dream of infinite and tender clemency. There was no frown, no wrinkle on its face, not a ripple. And the run of the slight swell was so smooth that it resembled the graceful undulation of a piece of shimmering gray silk shot with gleams of green. We pulled an easy stroke; but when the master of the brig, after a glance over his shoulder, stood up with a low exclamation, my men feathered their oars instinctively, without an order, and the boat lost her way.

He was steadying himself on my shoulder with a strong grip, while his other arm, flung up rigidly, pointed a denunciatory finger at the immense tranquility of the ocean. After his first exclamation, which stopped the swing of our oars, he made no sound, but his whole attitude seemed to cry out an indignant "Behold!" . . . I could not imagine what vision of evil had come to him. I was startled, and the amazing energy of his immobilized gesture made my heart beat faster with the anticipation of something monstrous and unsuspected. The stillness around us became crushing.

For a moment the succession of silky undulations ran on innocently. I saw each of them swell up the misty line of the horizon, far, far away beyond the derelict brig, and the next moment, with a slight friendly toss of our boat, it had passed under us and was gone. The lulling cadence of the rise and fall, the invariable gentleness of this irresistible force, the great charm of the deep waters, warmed my breast deliciously, like the subtle poison of a love-potion. But all this lasted only a few soothing seconds before I jumped up too, making the boat roll like the veriest landlubber.

Something startling, mysterious, hastily confused, was taking place. I watched it with incredulous and fascinated awe, as one watches the confused, swift movements of some deed of violence done in the dark. As if at a given signal, the run of the smooth undulations seemed checked suddenly around the brig. By a strange optical delusion the whole sea appeared to rise upon her in one overwhelming heave of its silky surface, where in one spot a smother of foam broke out ferociously. And then the effort subsided. It was all over, and the smooth swell ran on as before from the horizon in uninterrupted cadence of motion, passing under us with a slight friendly toss of our boat. Far

away, where the brig had been, an angry white stain
undulating on the surface of steely-gray waters, shot
with gleams of green, diminished swiftly, without a
hiss, like a patch of pure snow melting in the sun. And
the great stillness after this initiation into the sea's
implacable hate seemed full of dread thoughts and
shadows of disaster.

"Gone!" ejaculated from the depths of his chest my
bowman in a final tone. He spat in his hands, and took
a better grip on his oar. The captain of the brig lowered
his rigid arm slowly, and looked at our faces in a
solemnly conscious silence, which called upon us to
share in his simple-minded, marveling awe. All at once
he sat down by my side, and leaned forward earnestly
at my boat's crew, who, swinging together in a long,
easy stroke, kept their eyes fixed upon him faithfully.

"No ship could have done so well," he addressed
them firmly, after a moment of strained silence, during
which he seemed with trembling lips to seek for words
fit to bear such high testimony. "She was small, but
she was good. I had no anxiety. She was strong. Last
voyage I had my wife and two children in her. No other
ship could have stood so long the weather she had to
live through for days and days before we got dismasted
a fortnight ago. She was fairly worn out, and that's all.
You may believe me. She lasted under us for days and
days, but she could not last forever. It was long enough.
I am glad it is over. No better ship was ever left to sink
at sea on such a day as this."

He was competent to pronounce the funereal ora-
tion of a ship, this son of ancient sea-folk, whose
national existence, so little stained by the excesses of
manly virtues, had demanded nothing but the merest
foothold from the earth. By the merits of his sea-wise
forefathers and by the artlessness of his heart, he was
made fit to deliver this excellent discourse. There was

nothing wanting in its orderly arrangement — neither piety nor faith, nor the tribute of praise due to the worthy dead, with the edifying recital of their achievement. She had lived, he had loved her; she had suffered, and he was glad she was at rest. It was an excellent discourse. And it was orthodox, too, in its fidelity to the cardinal article of a seaman's faith, of which it was a single-minded confession. "Ships are all right." They are. They who live with the sea have got to hold by that creed first and last; and it came to me, as I glanced at him sideways, that some men were not altogether unworthy in honor and conscience to pronounce the funereal eulogium of a ship's constancy in life and death.

After this, sitting by my side with his loosely-clasped hands hanging between his knees, he uttered no word, made no movement till the shadow of our ship's sails fell on the boat, when, at the loud cheer greeting the return of the victors with their prize, he lifted up his troubled face with a faint smile of pathetic indulgence. This smile of the worthy descendant of the most ancient sea-folk whose audacity and hardihood had left no trace of greatness and glory upon the waters, completed the cycle of my initiation. There was an infinite depth of hereditary wisdom in its pitying sadness. It made the hearty bursts of cheering sound like a childish noise of triumph. Our crew shouted with immense confidence — honest souls! As if anybody could ever make sure of having prevailed against the sea, which has betrayed so many ships of great "name," so many proud men, so many towering ambitions of fame, power, wealth, greatness!

As I brought the boat under the falls my captain, in high good-humor, leaned over, spreading his red and freckled elbows on the rail, and called down to me sarcastically, out of the depths of his cynic philosopher's beard:

"So you have brought the boat back after all, have you?"

Sarcasm was "his way," and the most that can be said for it is that it was natural. This did not make it lovable. But it is decorous and expedient to fall in with one's commander's way. "Yes. I brought the boat back all right, sir," I answered. And the good man believed me. It was not for him to discern upon me the marks of my recent initiation. And yet I was not exactly the same youngster who had taken the boat away — all impatience for a race against death, with the prize of nine men's lives at the end.

Already I looked with other eyes upon the sea. I knew it capable of betraying the generous ardor of youth as implacably as, indifferent to evil and good, it would have betrayed the basest greed or the noblest heroism. My conception of its magnanimous greatness was gone. And I looked upon the true sea — the sea that plays with men till their hearts are broken, and wears stout ships to death. Nothing can touch the brooding bitterness of its heart. Open to all and faithful to none, it exercises its fascination for the undoing of the best. To love it is not well. It knows no bond of plighted troth, no fidelity to misfortune, to long companionship, to long devotion. The promise it holds out perpetually is very great; but the only secret of its possession is strength, strength — the jealous, sleepless strength of a man guarding a coveted treasure within his gates.

Chapter XXXVII

The cradle of oversea traffic and of the art of naval combats, the Mediterranean, apart from all the associations of adventure and glory, the common heritage of all mankind, makes a tender appeal to a seaman. It has sheltered the infancy of his craft. He looks upon it as a man may look at a vast nursery in an old, old mansion where innumerable generations of his own people have learned to walk. I say his own people because, in a sense, all sailors belong to one family: all are descended from that adventurous and shaggy ancestor who, bestriding a shapeless log and paddling with a crooked branch, accomplished the first coasting-trip in a sheltered bay ringing with the admiring howls of his tribe. It is a matter of regret that all those brothers in craft and feeling, whose generations have learned to walk a ship's deck in that nursery, have been also more than once fiercely engaged in cutting each other's throats there. But life, apparently, has such exigencies. Without human propensity to murder and other sorts of unrighteousness there would have been no historical heroism. It is a consoling reflection. And then, if one examines impartially the deeds of violence, they appear of but small consequence. From Salamis to Actium, through Lepanto and the Nile to the naval massacre of Navarino, not to mention other armed encounters of lesser interest, all the blood heroically spilt into the Mediterranean has not stained with a single trail of purple the deep azure of its classic waters.

Of course, it may be argued that battles have shaped the destiny of mankind. The question whether they have shaped it well would remain open, however. But it would be hardly worth discussing. It is very probable that, had the Battle of Salamis never been fought, the face of the world would have been much as we behold it now, fashioned by the mediocre inspiration and the short-sighted labors of men. From a long and miserable experience of suffering, injustice, disgrace and aggression the nations of the earth are mostly swayed by fear — fear of the sort that a little cheap oratory turns easily to rage, hate, and violence. Innocent, guileless fear has been the cause of many wars. Not, of course, the fear of war itself, which, in the evolution of sentiments and ideas, has come to be regarded at last as a half-mystic and glorious ceremony with certain fashionable rites and preliminary incantations, wherein the conception of its true nature has been lost. To apprehend the true aspect, force, and morality of war as a natural function of mankind one requires a feather in the hair and a ring in the nose, or, better still, teeth filed to a point and a tattooed breast. Unfortunately, a return to such simple ornamentation is impossible. We are bound to the chariot of progress. There is no going back; and, as bad luck would have it, our civilization, which has done so much for the comfort and adornment of our bodies and the elevation of our minds, has made lawful killing frightfully and needlessly expensive.

The whole question of improved armaments has been approached by the governments of the earth in a spirit of nervous and unreflecting haste, whereas the right way was lying plainly before them, and had only to be pursued with calm determination. The learned vigils and labors of a certain class of inventors should have been rewarded with honorable liberality as justice demanded; and the bodies of the inventors should have been blown to pieces by means of their own perfected explosives and improved weapons with extreme publicity as the commonest prudence dictated. By this method the ardor of research in that direction would have been restrained without infringing the sacred privileges of science. For the lack of a little cool thinking in our guides and masters this course has not been followed, and a beautiful simplicity has been sacrificed for no real advantage. A frugal mind cannot defend itself from considerable bitterness when reflecting that at the Battle of Actium (which was fought for no less a stake than the dominion of the world) the fleet of Octavianus Caesar and the fleet of Antonius, including the Egyptian division and Cleopatra's galley with purple sails, probably cost less than two modern battleships, or, as the modern naval book-jargon has it, two capital units. But no amount of lubberly book-jargon can disguise a fact well calculated to afflict the soul of every sound economist. It is not likely that the Mediterranean will ever behold a battle with a greater issue; but when the time comes for another historical fight its bottom will be enriched as never before by a quantity of jagged scrap-iron, paid for at pretty nearly its weight of gold by the deluded populations inhabiting the isles and continents of this planet.

Chapter XXXVIII

*H*appy he who, like Ulysses, has made an adventurous voyage; and there is no such sea for adventurous voyages as the Mediterranean — the inland sea which the ancients looked upon as so vast and so full of wonders. And, indeed, it was terrible and wonderful; for it is we alone who, swayed by the audacity of our minds and the tremors of our hearts, are the sole artisans of all the wonder and romance of the world.

It was for the Mediterranean sailors that fair-haired sirens sang among the black rocks seething in white foam and mysterious voices spoke in the darkness above the moving wave — voices menacing, seductive, or prophetic, like that voice heard at the beginning of the Christian era by the master of an African vessel in the Gulf of Syrta, whose calm nights are full of strange murmurs and flitting shadows. It called him by name, bidding him go and tell all men that the great god Pan was dead. But the great legend of the Mediterranean, the legend of traditional song and grave history, lives, fascinating and immortal, in our minds.

The dark and fearful sea of the subtle Ulysses' wanderings, agitated by the wrath of Olympian gods, harboring on its isles the fury of strange monsters and the wiles of strange women; the highway of heroes and sages, of warriors, pirates, and saints; the workaday sea of Carthaginian merchants and the pleasure lake of the Roman Caesars, claims the veneration of every seaman as the historical home of that spirit of open defiance against the great waters of the earth which is the very soul of his calling. Issuing thence to the west and south, as a youth leaves the shelter of his parental house, this spirit found the way to the Indies, discovered the coasts of a new continent, and traversed at last the immensity of the great Pacific, rich in groups of islands remote and mysterious like the constellations of the sky.

The first impulse of navigation took its visible form in that tideless basin freed from hidden shoals and treacherous currents, as if in tender regard for the infancy of the art. The steep shores of the Mediterranean favored the beginners in one of humanity's most daring enterprises, and the enchanting inland sea of classic adventure has led mankind gently from headland to headland, from bay to bay, from island to island, out into the promise of world-wide oceans beyond the Pillars of Hercules.

Chapter XXXIX

The charm of the Mediterranean dwells in the unforgettable flavor of my early days, and to this hour this sea, upon which the Romans alone ruled without dispute, has kept for me the fascination of youthful romance. The very first Christmas night I ever spent away from land was employed in running before a Gulf of Lions gale, which made the old ship groan in every timber as she skipped before it over the short seas until we brought her to, battered and out of breath, under the lee of Majorca, where the smooth water was torn by fierce cat's-paws under a very stormy sky.

We — or, rather, they, for I had hardly had two glimpses of salt water in my life till then — kept her standing off and on all that day, while I listened for the first time with the curiosity of my tender years to the song of the wind in a ship's rigging. The monotonous and vibrating note was destined to grow into the intimacy of the heart, pass into blood and bone, accompany the thoughts and acts of two full decades, remain to haunt like a reproach the peace of the quiet fireside, and enter into the very texture of respectable dreams dreamed safely under a roof of rafters and tiles.

The wind was fair, but that day we ran no more.

The thing (I will not call her a ship twice in the same half-hour) leaked. She leaked fully, generously, over-flowingly, all over — like a basket. I took an enthusiastic part in the excitement caused by that last infirmity of noble ships, without concerning myself much with the why or the wherefore. The surmise of my maturer years is that, bored by her interminable life, the venerable antiquity was simply yawning with ennui at every seam. But at the time I did not know; I knew generally very little, and least of all what I was doing in that *Galere.*

I remember that, exactly as in the comedy of Molière, my uncle asked the precise question in the very words — not of my confidential valet, however, but across great distances of land, in a letter whose mocking but indulgent turn ill concealed his almost paternal anxi-ety. I fancy I tried to convey to him my (utterly un-founded) impression that the West Indies awaited my coming. I had to go there. It was a sort of mystic conviction — something in the nature of a call. But it was difficult to state intelligibly the grounds of this belief to that man of rigorous logic, if of infinite charity.

The truth must have been that, all unversed in the arts of the wily Greek, the deceiver of gods, the lover of strange women, the evoker of bloodthirsty shades, I yet longed for the beginning of my own obscure Odyssey, which, as was proper for a modern, should unroll its wonders and terrors beyond the Pillars of Hercules. The disdainful ocean did not open wide to swallow up my audacity, though the ship, the ridicu-lous and ancient *Galere* of my folly, the old, weary, disenchanted sugar-wagon, seemed extremely disposed to open out and swallow up as much salt water as she could hold. This, if less grandiose, would have been as final a catastrophe.

But no catastrophe occurred. I lived to watch on a strange shore a black and youthful Nausicaa, with a joyous train of attendant maidens, carrying baskets of linen to a clear stream overhung by the heads of slender palm trees. The vivid colors of their draped raiment and the gold of their earrings invested with a barbaric and regal magnificence their figures, stepping out freely in a shower of broken sunshine. The whiteness of their teeth was still more dazzling than the splendor of jewels at their ears. The shaded side of the ravine gleamed with their smiles. They were as unabashed as so many princesses, but, alas! not one of them was the daughter of a jet-black sovereign. Such was my abominable luck in being born by the mere hair's breadth of twenty-five centuries too late into a world where kings have been growing scarce with scandalous rapidity, while the few who remain have adopted the uninteresting manners and customs of simple millionaires. Obviously it was a vain hope in 187- to see the ladies of a royal household walk in checkered sunshine, with baskets of linen on their heads, to the banks of a clear stream overhung by the starry fronds of palm trees. It was a vain hope. If I did not ask myself whether, limited by such discouraging impossibilities, life were still worth living, it was only because I had then before me several other pressing questions, some of which have remained unanswered to this day. The resonant, laughing voices of these gorgeous maidens scared away the multitude of hummingbirds, whose delicate wings wreathed with the mist of their vibration the tops of flowering bushes.

No, they were not princesses. Their unrestrained laughter filling the hot, fern-clad ravine had a soulless limpidity, as of wild, inhuman dwellers in tropical woodlands. Following the example of certain prudent travelers, I withdrew unseen — and returned, not much wiser, to the Mediterranean, the sea of classic adventures.

Chapter XL

*I*t was written that there, in the nursery of our navigating ancestors, I should learn to walk in the ways of my craft and grow in the love of the sea, blind as young love often is, but absorbing and disinterested as all true love must be. I demanded nothing from it — not even adventure. In this I showed, perhaps, more intuitive wisdom than high self-denial. No adventure ever came to one for the asking. He who starts on a deliberate quest of adventure goes forth but to gather dead-sea fruit, unless, indeed, he be beloved of the gods and great amongst heroes, like that most excellent cavalier Don Quixote de la Mancha. By us ordinary mortals of a mediocre animus that is only too anxious to pass by wicked giants for so many honest windmills, adventures are entertained like visiting angels. They come upon our complacency unawares. As unbidden guests are apt to do, they often come at inconvenient times. And we are glad to let them go unrecognized, without any acknowledgment of so high a favor. After many years, on looking back from the middle turn of life's way at the events of the past, which, like a friendly crowd, seem to gaze sadly after us hastening towards the Cimmerian shore, we may see here and there, in the gray throng, some figure glowing with a faint radiance, as though it had caught all the light of our already crepuscular sky. And by this glow we may recognize the faces of our true adventures, of the once unbidden guests entertained unawares in our young days.

If the Mediterranean, the venerable (and sometimes atrociously ill-tempered) nurse of all navigators, was to rock my youth, the providing of the cradle necessary for that operation was entrusted by Fate to the most casual assemblage of irresponsible young men (all, however, older than myself) that, as if drunk with Provencal sunshine, frittered life away in joyous levity on the model of Balzac's "Histoire des Treize" qualified by a dash of romance *de cape et d'epee.*

She who was my cradle in those years had been built on the River of Savona by a famous builder of boats, was rigged in Corsica by another good man, and was described on her papers as a 'tartane' of sixty tons. In reality, she was a true balancelle, with two short masts raking forward and two curved yards, each as long as her hull; a true child of the Latin lake, with a spread of two enormous sails resembling the pointed wings on a sea-bird's slender body, and herself, like a bird indeed, skimming rather than sailing the seas.

Her name was the Tremolino. How is this to be translated? The Quiverer? What a name to give the pluckiest little craft that ever dipped her sides in angry foam! I had felt her, it is true, trembling for nights and days together under my feet, but it was with the high-strung tenseness of her faithful courage. In her short, but brilliant, career she has taught me nothing, but she has given me everything. I owe to her the awakened love for the sea that, with the quivering of her swift little body and the humming of the wind under the foot of her lateen sails, stole into my heart with a sort of gentle violence, and brought my imagination under its despotic sway. The Tremolino! To this day I cannot utter or even write that name without a strange tightening of the breast and the gasp of mingled delight and dread of one's first passionate experience.

Chapter XLI

*W*e four formed (to use a term well understood
nowadays in every social sphere) a "syndicate" owning
the Tremolino: an international and astonishing syndicate. And we were all ardent Royalists of the snow-
white Legitimist complexion — Heaven only knows
why! In all associations of men there is generally one
who, by the authority of age and of a more experienced
wisdom, imparts a collective character to the whole set.
If I mention that the oldest of us was very old, extremely old — nearly thirty years old — and that he used
to declare with gallant carelessness, "I live by my
sword," I think I have given enough information on
the score of our collective wisdom. He was a North
Carolinian gentleman, J. M. K. B. were the initials of
his name, and he really did live by the sword, as far as
I know. He died by it, too, later on, in a Balkanian
squabble, in the cause of some Serbs or else Bulgarians,
who were neither Catholics nor gentlemen — at least,
not in the exalted but narrow sense he attached to that
last word.

Poor J. M. K. B., *Americain, Catholique, Et Gentil-
homme,* as he was disposed to describe himself in mo-

ments of lofty expansion! Are there still to be found in Europe gentlemen keen of face and elegantly slight of body, of distinguished aspect, with a fascinating drawing room manner and with a dark, fatal glance, who live by their swords, I wonder? His family had been ruined in the Civil War, I fancy, and seems for a decade or so to have led a wandering life in the Old World. As to Henry C——, the next in age and wisdom of our band, he had broken loose from the unyielding rigidity of his family, solidly rooted, if I remember rightly, in a well-to-do London suburb. On their respectable authority he introduced himself meekly to strangers as a "black sheep." I have never seen a more guileless specimen of an outcast. Never.

However, his people had the grace to send him a little money now and then. Enamored of the South, of Provence, of its people, its life, its sunshine and its poetry, narrow-chested, tall and short-sighted, he strode along the streets and the lanes, his long feet projecting far in advance of his body, and his white nose and gingery moustache buried in an open book: for he had the habit of reading as he walked. How he avoided falling into precipices, off the quays, or down staircases is a great mystery. The sides of his overcoat bulged out with pocket editions of various poets. When not engaged in reading Virgil, Homer, or Mistral, in parks, restaurants, streets, and suchlike public places, he indited sonnets (in French) to the eyes, ears, chin, hair, and other visible perfections of a nymph called Therese, the daughter, honesty compels me to state, of a certain Madame Leonore who kept a small café for sailors in one of the narrowest streets of the old town.

No more charming face, clear-cut like an antique gem, and delicate in coloring like the petal of a flower, had ever been set on, alas! a somewhat squat body. He read his verses aloud to her in the very café with the innocence of a little child and the vanity of a poet. We followed him there willingly enough, if only to watch the divine Therese laugh, under the vigilant black eyes of Madame Leonore, her mother. She laughed very prettily, not so much at the sonnets, which she could not but esteem, as at poor Henry's French accent, which was unique, resembling the warbling of birds, if birds ever warbled with a stuttering, nasal intonation.

Our third partner was Roger P. de la S——, the most Scandinavian-looking of Provencal squires, fair, and six feet high, as became a descendant of sea-roving Northmen, authoritative, incisive, wittily scornful, with a comedy in three acts in his pocket, and in his breast a heart blighted by a hopeless passion for his beautiful cousin, married to a wealthy hide and tallow merchant. He used to take us to lunch at their house without ceremony. I admired the good lady's sweet patience. The husband was a conciliatory soul, with a great fund of resignation, which he expended on "Roger's friends." I suspect he was secretly horrified at these invasions. But it was a Carlist salon, and as such we were made welcome. The possibility of raising Catalonia in the interest of the *Rey Netto*, who had just then crossed the Pyrenees, was much discussed there.

Don Carlos, no doubt, must have had many queer friends (it is the common lot of all Pretenders), but amongst them none more extravagantly fantastic than the Tremolino Syndicate, which used to meet in a tavern on the quays of the old port. The antique city of Massilia had surely never, since the days of the earliest Phoenicians, known an odder set of ship-owners. We met to discuss and settle the plan of operations for each voyage of the Tremolino. In these operations a banking-house, too, was concerned — a very respectable banking-house. But I am afraid I shall end by saying too much. Ladies, too, were concerned (I am really afraid I am saying too much) — all sorts of ladies, some old enough to know better than to put their trust in princes, others young and full of illusions.

One of these last was extremely amusing in the imitations, she gave us in confidence, of various highly-placed personages she was perpetually rushing off to Paris to interview in the interests of the cause — *Por El Rey!* For she was a Carlist, and of Basque blood at that, with something of a lioness in the expression of her courageous face (especially when she let her hair down), and with the volatile little soul of a sparrow dressed in fine Parisian feathers, which had the trick of coming off disconcertingly at unexpected moments.

But her imitations of a Parisian personage, very highly placed indeed, as she represented him standing in the corner of a room with his face to the wall, rubbing the back of his head and moaning helplessly, "Rita, you are the death of me!" were enough to make one (if young and free from cares) split one's sides laughing. She had an uncle still living, a very effective Carlist, too, the priest of a little mountain parish in Guipuzcoa. As the sea-going member of the syndicate (whose plans depended greatly on Dona Rita's information), I used to be charged with humbly affectionate messages for the old man. These messages I was supposed to deliver to the Arragonese muleteers (who were sure to await at certain times the Tremolino in the neighborhood of the Gulf of Rosas), for faithful transportation inland, together with the various unlawful goods landed secretly from under the Tremolino's hatches.

Well, now, I have really let out too much (as I feared I should in the end) as to the usual contents of my sea-cradle. But let it stand. And if anybody remarks cynically that I must have been a promising infant in those days, let that stand, too. I am concerned but for the good name of the Tremolino, and I affirm that a ship is ever guiltless of the sins, transgressions, and follies of her men.

Chapter XLII

*I*t was not Tremolino's fault that the syndicate depended so much on the wit and wisdom and the information of Dona Rita. She had taken a little furnished house on the Prado for the good of the cause — *Por El Rey!* She was always taking little houses for somebody's good, for the sick or the sorry, for broken-down artists, cleaned-out gamblers, temporarily unlucky speculators — *Vieux Amis* — old friends, as she used to explain apologetically, with a shrug of her fine shoulders.

Whether Don Carlos was one of the "old friends," too, it's hard to say. More unlikely things have been heard of in smoking-rooms. All I know is that one evening, entering incautiously the salon of the little house just after the news of a considerable Carlist success had reached the faithful, I was seized round the neck and waist and whirled recklessly three times round the room, to the crash of upsetting furniture and the humming of a valse tune in a warm contralto voice.

When released from the dizzy embrace, I sat down on the carpet — suddenly, without affectation. In this unpretentious attitude I became aware that J. M. K. B. had followed me into the room, elegant, fatal, correct and severe in a white tie and large shirt-front. In answer to his politely sinister, prolonged glance of inquiry, I overheard Dona Rita murmuring, with some confusion and annoyance, *"Vous etes bete mon cher. Voyons! Ca n'a aucune consequence."* Well content in this case to be of no particular consequence, I had already about me the elements of some worldly sense.

Rearranging my collar, which, truth to say, ought to have been a round one above a short jacket, but was not, I observed felicitously that I had come to say good-bye, being ready to go off to sea that very night with the Tremolino. Our hostess, slightly panting yet, and just a shade disheveled, turned tartly upon J. M. K. B., desiring to know when *he* would be ready to go off by the Tremolino, or in any other way, in order to join the royal headquarters. Did he intend, she asked ironically, to wait for the very eve of the entry into Madrid? Thus by a judicious exercise of tact and asperity we re-established the atmospheric equilibrium of the room long before I left them a little before midnight, now tenderly reconciled, to walk down to the harbor and hail the Tremolino by the usual soft whistle from the edge of the quay. It was our signal, invariably heard by the ever-watchful Dominic, the *Padrone.*

He would raise a lantern silently to light my steps along the narrow, springy plank of our primitive gangway. "And so we are going off," he would murmur directly my foot touched the deck. I was the harbinger of sudden departures, but there was nothing in the world sudden enough to take Dominic unawares. His thick black moustaches, curled every morning with hot tongs by the barber at the corner of the quay, seemed to hide a perpetual smile. But nobody, I believe, had ever seen the true shape of his lips. From the slow,

imperturbable gravity of that broad-chested man you
would think he had never smiled in his life. In his eyes
lurked a look of perfectly remorseless irony, as though
he had been provided with an extremely experienced
soul; and the slightest distension of his nostrils would
give to his bronzed face a look of extraordinary bold-
ness. This was the only play of feature of which he
seemed capable, being a Southerner of a concentrated,
deliberate type. His ebony hair curled slightly on the
temples. He may have been forty years old, and he was
a great voyager on the inland sea.

Astute and ruthless, he could have rivaled in resource
the unfortunate son of Laertes and Anticlea. If he did
not pit his craft and audacity against the very gods, it
is only because the Olympian gods are dead. Certainly
no woman could frighten him. A one-eyed giant would
not have had the ghost of a chance against Dominic
Cervoni, of Corsica, not Ithaca; and no king, son of
kings, but of very respectable family — authentic
Caporali, he affirmed. But that is as it may be. The
Caporali families date back to the twelfth century.

For want of more exalted adversaries Dominic
turned his audacity fertile in impious stratagems
against the powers of the earth, as represented by the
institution of Custom-houses and every mortal belonging thereto — scribes, officers, and guardacostas afloat
and ashore. He was the very man for us, this modern
and unlawful wanderer with his own legend of loves,
dangers, and bloodshed. He told us bits of it sometimes in measured, ironic tones. He spoke Catalonian,
the Italian of Corsica and the French of Provence with
the same easy naturalness. Dressed in shore-togs, a
white starched shirt, black jacket, and round hat, as I
took him once to see Dona Rita, he was extremely
presentable. He could make himself interesting by a
tactful and rugged reserve set off by a grim, almost

imperceptible, playfulness of tone and manner.

He had the physical assurance of strong-hearted men. After half an hour's interview in the dining room, during which they got in touch with each other in an amazing way, Rita told us in her best *Grande Dame* manner: *"Mais il esi parfait, cet homme."* He was perfect. On board the Tremolino, wrapped up in a black *caban,* the picturesque cloak of Mediterranean seamen, with those massive moustaches and his remorseless eyes set off by the shadow of the deep hood, he looked piratical and monkish and darkly initiated into the most awful mysteries of the sea.

Chapter XLIII

*A*nyway, he was perfect, as Dona Rita had declared. The only thing unsatisfactory (and even inexplicable) about our Dominic was his nephew, Cesar. It was startling to see a desolate expression of shame veil the remorseless audacity in the eyes of that man superior to all scruples and terrors.

"I would never have dared to bring him on board your balancelle," he once apologized to me. "But what am I to do? His mother is dead, and my brother has gone into the bush."

In this way I learned that our Dominic had a brother. As to "going into the bush," this only means that a man has done his duty successfully in the pursuit of a hereditary vendetta. The feud which had existed for ages between the families of Cervoni and Brunaschi was so old that it seemed to have smoldered out at last. One evening Pietro Brunaschi, after a laborious day amongst his olive trees, sat on a chair against the wall of his house with a bowl of broth on his knees and a piece of bread in his hand. Dominic's brother, going home with a gun on his shoulder, found a sudden offence in this picture of content and rest so obviously calculated to awaken the feelings of hatred and revenge. He and Pietro had never had any personal quarrel; but, as Dominic explained, "all our dead cried out to him." He shouted from behind a wall of stones, "O Pietro! Behold what is coming!" And as the other looked up innocently he took aim at the forehead and squared the old vendetta account so neatly that, according to Dominic, the dead man continued to sit with the bowl of broth on his knees and the piece of bread in his hand.

This is why — because in Corsica your dead will not leave you alone — Dominic's brother had to go into the *Maquis*, into the bush on the wild mountainside, to dodge the gendarmes for the insignificant remainder of his life, and Dominic had charge of his nephew with a mission to make a man of him.

No more unpromising undertaking could be imagined. The very material for the task seemed wanting. The Cervonis, if not handsome men, were good sturdy flesh and blood. But this extraordinarily lean and livid youth seemed to have no more blood in him than a snail.

"Some cursed witch must have stolen my brother's child from the cradle and put that spawn of a starved devil in its place," Dominic would say to me. "Look at him! Just look at him!"

To look at Cesar was not pleasant. His parchment skin, showing dead white on his cranium through the thin wisps of dirty brown hair, seemed to be glued directly and tightly upon his big bones, Without being in any way deformed, he was the nearest approach which I have ever seen or could imagine to what is commonly understood by the word "monster." That the source of the effect produced was really moral I have no doubt. An utterly, hopelessly depraved nature was expressed in physical terms, that taken each separately had nothing positively startling. You imagined him clammily cold to the touch, like a snake. The slightest reproof, the most mild and justifiable remonstrance, would be met by a resentful glare and an evil shrinking of his thin dry upper lip, a snarl of hate to which he generally added the agreeable sound of grinding teeth.

It was for this venomous performance rather than for his lies, impudence, and laziness that his uncle used to knock him down. It must not be imagined that it was anything in the nature of a brutal assault. Dominic's brawny arm would be seen describing deliberately an ample horizontal gesture, a dignified sweep, and Cesar would go over suddenly like a ninepin — which was funny to see. But, once down, he would writhe on the deck, gnashing his teeth in impotent rage — which was pretty horrible to behold. And it also happened more than once that he would disappear completely — which was startling to observe. This is the exact truth. Before some of these majestic cuffs Cesar would go down and vanish. He would vanish heels overhead into open hatchways, into scuttles, behind up-ended casks, according to the place where he happened to come into contact with his uncle's mighty arm.

Once — it was in the old harbor, just before the Tremolino's last voyage — he vanished thus overboard to my infinite consternation. Dominic and I had been talking business together aft, and Cesar had sneaked up behind us to listen, for, amongst his other perfections, he was a consummate eavesdropper and spy. At the sound of the heavy plop alongside horror held me rooted to the spot; but Dominic stepped quietly to the rail and leaned over, waiting for his nephew's miserable head to bob up for the first time.

"Ohe, Cesar!" he yelled contemptuously to the spluttering wretch. "Catch hold of that mooring hawser — *charogne!*"

He approached me to resume the interrupted conversation.

"What about Cesar?" I asked anxiously.

"Canallia! Let him hang there," was his answer. And he went on talking over the business in hand calmly, while I tried vainly to dismiss from my mind the picture of Cesar steeped to the chin in the water of the old harbor, a decoction of centuries of marine refuse. I tried to dismiss it, because the mere notion of that liquid made me feel very sick. Presently Dominic, hailing an idle boatman, directed him to go and fish his nephew out; and by-and-by Cesar appeared walking on board from the quay, shivering, streaming with filthy water, with bits of rotten straws in his hair and a piece of dirty orange-peel stranded on his shoulder. His teeth chattered; his yellow eyes squinted balefully at us as he passed forward. I thought it my duty to remonstrate.

"Why are you always knocking him about, Dominic?" I asked. Indeed, I felt convinced it was no earthly good — a sheer waste of muscular force.

"I must try to make a man of him," Dominic answered hopelessly.

I restrained the obvious retort that in this way he ran the risk of making, in the words of the immortal Mr. Mantalini, "a demnition damp, unpleasant corpse of him."

"He wants to be a locksmith!" burst out Cervoni. "To learn how to pick locks, I suppose," he added with sardonic bitterness.

"Why not let him be a locksmith?" I ventured.

"Who would teach him?" he cried. "Where could I leave him?" he asked, with a drop in his voice; and I had my first glimpse of genuine despair. "He steals, you know, alas! *Par ta madonne!* I believe he would put poison in your food and mine — the viper!"

He raised his face and both his clenched fists slowly to heaven. However, Cesar never dropped poison into our cups. One cannot be sure, but I fancy he went to work in another way.

This voyage, of which the details need not be given, we had to range far afield for sufficient reasons. Coming up from the South to end it with the important and really dangerous part of the scheme in hand, we found it necessary to look into Barcelona for certain definite information. This appears like running one's head into the very jaws of the lion, but in reality it was not so. We had one or two high, influential friends there, and many others humble but valuable because bought for good hard cash. We were in no danger of being molested; indeed, the important information reached us promptly by the hands of a Custom-house officer, who came on board full of showy zeal to poke an iron rod into the layer of oranges which made the visible part of our cargo in the hatchway.

I forgot to mention before that the Tremolino was officially known as a fruit and cork-wood trader. The zealous officer managed to slip a useful piece of paper into Dominic's hand as he went ashore, and a few hours afterwards, being off duty, he returned on board again athirst for drinks and gratitude. He got both as a matter of course. While he sat sipping his liqueur in the tiny cabin, Dominic plied him with questions as to the whereabouts of the guardacostas. The preventive service afloat was really the one for us to reckon with, and it was material for our success and safety to know the exact position of the patrol craft in the neighborhood. The news could not have been more favorable. The officer mentioned a small place on the coast some twelve miles off, where, unsuspicious and unready, she was lying at anchor, with her sails unbent, painting yards and scraping spars. Then he left us after the usual compliments, smirking reassurringly over his shoulder.

I had kept below pretty close all day from excess of prudence. The stake played on that trip was big.

"We are ready to go at once, but for Cesar, who has been missing ever since breakfast," announced Dominic to me in his slow, grim way.

Where the fellow had gone, and why, we could not imagine. The usual surmises in the case of a missing seaman did not apply to Cesar's absence. He was too odious for love, friendship, gambling, or even casual intercourse. But once or twice he had wandered away like this before.

Dominic went ashore to look for him, but returned at the end of two hours alone and very angry, as I could see by the token of the invisible smile under his moustache being intensified. We wondered what had become of the wretch, and made a hurried investigation amongst our portable property. He had stolen nothing.

"He will be back before long," I said confidently.

Ten minutes afterwards one of the men on deck called out loudly:

"I can see him coming."

Cesar had only his shirt and trousers on. He had sold his coat, apparently for pocket-money.

"You knave!" was all Dominic said, with a terrible softness of voice. He restrained his choler for a time. "Where have you been, vagabond?" he asked menacingly.

Nothing would induce Cesar to answer that question. It was as if he even disdained to lie. He faced us, drawing back his lips and gnashing his teeth, and did not shrink an inch before the sweep of Dominic's arm.

He went down as if shot, of course. But this time I noticed that, when picking himself up, he remained longer than usual on all fours, baring his big teeth over his shoulder and glaring upwards at his uncle with a new sort of hate in his round, yellow eyes. That permanent sentiment seemed pointed at that moment by especial malice and curiosity. I became quite interested. If he ever manages to put poison in the dishes, I thought to myself, this is how he will look at us as we sit at our meal. But I did not, of course, believe for a moment that he would ever put poison in our food. He ate the same things himself. Moreover, he had no poison. And I could not imagine a human being so blinded by cupidity as to sell poison to such an atrocious creature.

Chapter XLIV

We slipped out to sea quietly at dusk, and all through the night everything went well. The breeze was gusty; a southerly blow was making up. It was fair wind for our course. Now and then Dominic slowly and rhythmically struck his hands together a few times, as if applauding the performance of the Tremolino. The balancelle hummed and quivered as she flew along, dancing lightly under our feet.

At daybreak I pointed out to Dominic, amongst the several sail in view running before the gathering storm, one particular vessel. The press of canvas she carried made her loom up high, end-on, like a gray column standing motionless directly in our wake.

"Look at this fellow, Dominic," I said. "He seems to be in a hurry."

The Padrone made no remark, but, wrapping his black cloak close about him, stood up to look. His weather-tanned face, framed in the hood, had an aspect of authority and challenging force, with the deep-set eyes gazing far away fixedly, without a wink, like the intent, merciless, steady eyes of a sea-bird.

"*Chi va piano va sano,*" he remarked at last, with a

derisive glance over the side, in ironic allusion to our own tremendous speed.

The Tremolino was doing her best, and seemed to hardly touch the great burst of foam over which she darted. I crouched down again to get some shelter from the low bulwark. After more than half an hour of swaying immobility expressing a concentrated, breathless watchfulness, Dominic sank on the deck by my side. Within the monkish cowl his eyes gleamed with a fierce expression which surprised me. All he said was:

"He has come out here to wash the new paint off his yards, I suppose."

"What?" I shouted, getting up on my knees. "Is she the guardacosta?"

The perpetual suggestion of a smile under Dominic's piratical moustaches seemed to become more accentuated — quite real, grim, actually almost visible through the wet and uncurled hair. Judging by that symptom, he must have been in a towering rage. But I could also see that he was puzzled, and that discovery affected me disagreeably. Dominic puzzled! For a long time, leaning against the bulwark, I gazed over the stern at the gray column that seemed to stand swaying slightly in our wake always at the same distance.

Meanwhile Dominic, black and cowled, sat cross-legged on the deck, with his back to the wind, recalling vaguely an Arab chief in his burnuss sitting on the sand. Above his motionless figure the little cord and tassel on the stiff point of the hood swung about inanely in the gale. At last I gave up facing the wind and rain, and crouched down by his side. I was satisfied that the sail was a patrol craft. Her presence was not a thing to talk about, but soon, between two clouds charged with hail-showers, a burst of sunshine fell upon her sails, and our men discovered her character for themselves. From that moment I noticed that they seemed to take no heed of each other or of anything else. They could spare no eyes and no thought but for the slight column-shape astern of us. Its swaying had become perceptible. For a moment she remained dazzlingly white, then faded away slowly to nothing in a squall, only to reappear again, nearly black, resembling a post stuck upright against the slaty background of solid cloud. Since first noticed she had not gained on us a foot.

"She will never catch the Tremolino," I said exultingly.

Dominic did not look at me. He remarked absently, but justly, that the heavy weather was in our pursuer's favor. She was three times our size. What we had to do was to keep our distance till dark, which we could manage easily, and then haul off to seaward and consider the situation. But his thoughts seemed to stumble in the darkness of some not-solved enigma, and soon he fell silent. We ran steadily, wing-and-wing. Cape San Sebastian nearly ahead seemed to recede from us in the squalls of rain, and come out again to meet our rush, every time more distinct between the showers.

For my part I was by no means certain that this *Gabelou* (as our men alluded to her opprobriously) was after us at all. There were nautical difficulties in such a view which made me express the sanguine opinion that she was in all innocence simply changing her station. At this Dominic condescended to turn his head.

"I tell you she is in chase," he affirmed moodily, after one short glance astern.

I never doubted his opinion. But with all the ardor of a neophyte and the pride of an apt learner I was at that time a great nautical casuist.

"What I can't understand," I insisted subtly, "is how

on earth, with this wind, she has managed to be just where she was when we first made her out. It is clear that she could not, and did not, gain twelve miles on us during the night. And there are other impossibilities. . . ."

Dominic had been sitting motionless, like an inanimate black cone posed on the stern deck, near the rudder-head, with a small tassel fluttering on its sharp point, and for a time he preserved the immobility of his meditation. Then, bending over with a short laugh, he gave my ear the bitter fruit of it. He understood everything now perfectly. She was where we had seen her first, not because she had caught us up, but because we had passed her during the night while she was already waiting for us, hove-to, most likely, on our very track.

"Do you understand — already?" Dominic muttered in a fierce undertone. "Already! You know we left a good eight hours before we were expected to leave, otherwise she would have been in time to lie in wait for us on the other side of the Cape, and" — he snapped his teeth like a wolf close to my face — "and she would have had us like — that."

I saw it all plainly enough now. They had eyes in their heads and all their wits about them in that craft. We had passed them in the dark as they jogged on easily towards their ambush with the idea that we were yet far behind. At daylight, however, sighting a balancelle ahead under a press of canvas, they had made sail in chase. But if that was so, then —

Dominic seized my arm.

"Yes, yes! She came out on an information — do you see, it? — on information. . . . We have been sold — betrayed. Why? How? What for? We always paid them all so well on shore. . . . No! But it is my head that is going to burst."

He seemed to choke, tugged at the throat button of the cloak, jumped up open-mouthed as if to hurl curses and denunciation, but instantly mastered himself, and, wrapping up the cloak closer about him, sat down on the deck again as quiet as ever.

"Yes, it must be the work of some scoundrel ashore," I observed.

He pulled the edge of the hood well forward over his brow before he muttered:

"A scoundrel. . . . Yes. . . . It's evident."

"Well," I said, "they can't get us, that's clear."

"No," he assented quietly, "they cannot."

We shaved the Cape very close to avoid an adverse current. On the other side, by the effect of the land, the wind failed us so completely for a moment that the Tremolino's two great lofty sails hung idle to the masts in the thundering uproar of the seas breaking upon the shore we had left behind. And when the returning gust filled them again, we saw with amazement half of the new mainsail, which we thought fit to drive the boat under before giving way, absolutely fly out of the bolt-ropes. We lowered the yard at once, and saved it all, but it was no longer a sail; it was only a heap of soaked strips of canvas cumbering the deck and weighting the craft. Dominic gave the order to throw the whole lot overboard.

I would have had the yard thrown overboard, too, he said, leading me aft again, "if it had not been for the trouble. Let no sign escape you," he continued, lowering his voice, "but I am going to tell you something terrible. Listen: I have observed that the roping stitches on that sail have been cut! You hear? Cut with a knife in many places. And yet it stood all that time. Not enough cut. That flap did it at last. What matters it? But look! there's treachery seated on this very deck. By the horns of the devil! seated here at our very backs.

Do not turn, signorine."

We were facing aft then.

"What's to be done?" I asked, appalled.

"Nothing. Silence! Be a man, signorine."

"What else?" I said.

To show I could be a man, I resolved to utter no sound as long as Dominic himself had the force to keep his lips closed. Nothing but silence becomes certain situations. Moreover, the experience of treachery seemed to spread a hopeless drowsiness over my thoughts and senses. For an hour or more we watched our pursuer surging out nearer and nearer from amongst the squalls that sometimes hid her altogether. But even when not seen, we felt her there like a knife at our throats. She gained on us frightfully. And the Tremolino, in a fierce breeze and in much smoother water, swung on easily under her one sail, with something appallingly careless in the joyous freedom of her motion. Another half-hour went by. I could not stand it any longer.

"They will get the poor barky," I stammered out suddenly, almost on the verge of tears.

Dominic stirred no more than a carving. A sense of catastrophic loneliness overcame my inexperienced soul. The vision of my companions passed before me. The whole Royalist gang was in Monte Carlo now, I reckoned. And they appeared to me clear-cut and very small, with affected voices and stiff gestures, like a procession of rigid marionettes upon a toy stage. I gave a start. What was this? A mysterious, remorseless whisper came from within the motionless black hood at my side.

"*Il faut la tuer.*"

I heard it very well.

"What do you say, Dominic?" I asked, moving nothing but my lips.

And the whisper within the hood repeated mysteriously, "She must be killed."

My heart began to beat violently.

"That's it," I faltered out. "But how?"

"You love her well?"

"I do."

"Then you must find the heart for that work too. You must steer her yourself, and I shall see to it that she dies quickly, without leaving as much as a chip behind."

"Can you?" I murmured, fascinated by the black hood turned immovably over the stern, as if in unlawful communion with that old sea of magicians, slave-dealers, exiles and warriors, the sea of legends and terrors, where the mariners of remote antiquity used to hear the restless shade of an old wanderer weep aloud in the dark.

"I know a rock," whispered the initiated voice within the hood secretly. "But — caution! It must be done before our men perceive what we are about. Whom can we trust now? A knife drawn across the fore halyards would bring the foresail down, and put an end to our liberty in twenty minutes. And the best of our men may be afraid of drowning. There is our little boat, but in an affair like this no one can be sure of being saved."

The voice ceased. We had started from Barcelona with our dinghy in tow; afterwards it was too risky to try to get her in, so we let her take her chance of the seas at the end of a comfortable scope of rope. Many times she had seemed to us completely overwhelmed, but soon we would see her bob up again on a wave, apparently as buoyant and whole as ever.

"I understand," I said softly. "Very well, Dominic. When?"

"Not yet. We must get a little more in first," answered the voice from the hood in a ghostly murmur.

Chapter XLV

*I*t was settled. I had now the courage to turn about. Our men crouched about the decks here and there with anxious, crestfallen faces, all turned one way to watch the chaser. For the first time that morning I perceived Cesar stretched out full length on the deck near the foremast and wondered where he had been skulking till then. But he might in truth have been at my elbow all the time for all I knew. We had been too absorbed in watching our fate to pay attention to each other. Nobody had eaten anything that morning, but the men had been coming constantly to drink at the water-butt.

I ran down to the cabin. I had there, put away in a locker, ten thousand francs in gold of whose presence on board, so far as I was aware, not a soul, except Dominic had the slightest inkling. When I emerged on deck again Dominic had turned about and was peering from under his cowl at the coast. Cape Creux closed the view ahead. To the left a wide bay, its waters torn and swept by fierce squalls, seemed full of smoke. Astern the sky had a menacing look.

Directly he saw me, Dominic, in a placid tone,

wanted to know what was the matter. I came close to
him and, looking as unconcerned as I could, told him
in an undertone that I had found the locker broken
open and the money-belt gone. Last evening it was still
there.

"What did you want to do with it?" he asked me,
trembling violently.

"Put it round my waist, of course," I answered,
amazed to hear his teeth chattering.

"Cursed gold!" he muttered. "The weight of the
money might have cost you your life, perhaps." He
shuddered. "There is no time to talk about that now."

"I am ready."

"Not yet. I am waiting for that squall to come over,"
he muttered. And a few leaden minutes passed.

The squall came over at last. Our pursuer, overtaken
by a sort of murky whirlwind, disappeared from our
sight. The Tremolino quivered and bounded forward.
The land ahead vanished, too, and we seemed to be left
alone in a world of water and wind.

"*Prenez la barre, Monsieur,*" Dominic broke the silence
suddenly in an austere voice. "Take hold of the tiller."
He bent his hood to my ear. "The balancelle is yours.
Your own hands must deal the blow. I — I have yet
another piece of work to do." He spoke up loudly to
the man who steered. "Let the signorino take the tiller,
and you with the others stand by to haul the boat
alongside quickly at the word."

The man obeyed, surprised, but silent. The others
stirred, and pricked up their ears at this. I heard their
murmurs. "What now? Are we going to run in somewhere and take to our heels? The Padrone knows what
he is doing."

Dominic went forward. He paused to look down at
Cesar, who, as I have said before, was lying full length
face down by the foremast, then stepped over him, and

dived out of my sight under the foresail. I saw nothing ahead. It was impossible for me to see anything except the foresail open and still, like a great shadowy wing. But Dominic had his bearings. His voice came to me from forward, in a just audible cry:

"Now, signorino!"

I bore on the tiller, as instructed before. Again I heard him faintly, and then I had only to hold her straight. No ship ran so joyously to her death before. She rose and fell, as if floating in space, and darted forward, whizzing like an arrow. Dominic, stooping under the foot of the foresail, reappeared, and stood steadying himself against the mast, with a raised forefinger in an attitude of expectant attention. A second before the shock his arm fell down by his side. At that I set my teeth. And then —

Talk of splintered planks and smashed timbers! This shipwreck lies upon my soul with the dread and horror of a homicide, with the unforgettable remorse of having crushed a living, faithful heart at a single blow. At one moment the rush and the soaring swing of speed; the next a crash, and death, stillness — a moment of horrible immobility, with the song of the wind changed to a strident wail, and the heavy waters boiling up menacing and sluggish around the corpse. I saw in a distracting minute the foreyard fly fore and aft with a brutal swing, the men all in a heap, cursing with fear, and hauling frantically at the line of the boat. With a strange welcoming of the familiar I saw also Cesar amongst them, and recognized Dominic's old, well-known, effective gesture, the horizontal sweep of his powerful arm. I recollect distinctly saying to myself, "Cesar must go down, of course," and then, as I was scrambling on all fours, the swinging tiller I had let go caught me a crack under the ear, and knocked me over senseless.

I don't think I was actually unconscious for more than a few minutes, but when I came to myself the dinghy was driving before the wind into a sheltered cove, two men just keeping her straight with their oars. Dominic, with his arm round my shoulders, supported me in the stern-sheets.

We landed in a familiar part of the country. Dominic took one of the boat's oars with him. I suppose he was thinking of the stream we would have presently to cross, on which there was a miserable specimen of a punt, often robbed of its pole. But first of all we had to ascend the ridge of land at the back of the Cape. He helped me up. I was dizzy. My head felt very large and heavy. At the top of the ascent I clung to him, and we stopped to rest.

To the right, below us, the wide, smoky bay was empty. Dominic had kept his word. There was not a chip to be seen around the black rock from which the Tremolino, with her plucky heart crushed at one blow, had slipped off into deep water to her eternal rest. The vastness of the open sea was smothered in driving mists, and in the center of the thinning squall, phantomlike, under a frightful press of canvas, the unconscious guardacosta dashed on, still chasing to the northward. Our men were already descending the reverse slope to look for that punt which we knew from experience was not always to be found easily. I looked after them with dazed, misty eyes. One, two, three, four.

"Dominic, where's Cesar?" I cried.

As if repulsing the very sound of the name, the Padrone made that ample, sweeping, knocking-down gesture. I stepped back a pace and stared at him fearfully. His open shirt uncovered his muscular neck and the thick hair on his chest. He planted the oar upright in the soft soil, and rolling up slowly his right sleeve, extended the bare arm before my face.

"This," he began, with an extreme deliberation, whose superhuman restraint vibrated with the suppressed violence of his feelings, "is the arm which delivered the blow. I am afraid it is your own gold that did the rest. I forgot all about your money." He clasped his hands together in sudden distress. "I forgot, I forgot," he repeated disconsolately.

"Cesar stole the belt?" I stammered out, bewildered.

"And who else? *Canallia!* He must have been spying on you for days. And he did the whole thing. Absent all day in Barcelona. *Traditore!* Sold his jacket — to hire a horse. Ha! ha! A good affair! I tell you it was he who set him at us. . . ."

Dominic pointed at the sea, where the guardacosta was a mere dark speck. His chin dropped on his breast.

". . . On information," he murmured, in a gloomy voice. "A Cervoni! Oh! my poor brother. . . !"

"And you drowned him," I said feebly.

"I struck once, and the wretch went down like a stone — with the gold. Yes. But he had time to read in my eyes that nothing could save him while I was alive. And had I not the right — I, Dominic Cervoni, Padrone, who brought him aboard your fellucca — my nephew, a traitor?"

He pulled the oar out of the ground and helped me carefully down the slope. All the time he never once looked me in the face. He punted us over, then shouldered the oar again and waited till our men were at some distance before he offered me his arm. After we had gone a little way, the fishing hamlet we were making for came into view. Dominic stopped.

"Do you think you can make your way as far as the houses by yourself?" he asked me quietly.

"Yes, I think so. But why? Where are you going, Dominic?"

"Anywhere. What a question! Signorino, you are but

little more than a boy to ask such a question of a man having this tale in his family. *Ah! Traditore!* What made me ever own that spawn of a hungry devil for our own blood! Thief, cheat, coward, liar — other men can deal with that. But I was his uncle, and so . . . I wish he had poisoned me — *Charogne!* But this: that I, a confidential man and a Corsican, should have to ask your pardon for bringing on board your vessel, of which I was Padrone, a Cervoni, who has betrayed you — a traitor! — that is too much. It is too much. Well, I beg your pardon; and you may spit in Dominic's face because a traitor of our blood taints us all. A theft may be made good between men, a lie may be set right, a death avenged, but what can one do to atone for a treachery like this. . . ? Nothing."

He turned and walked away from me along the bank of the stream, flourishing a vengeful arm and repeating to himself slowly, with savage emphasis: *"Ah! Canaille! Canaille! Canaille. . . !"* He left me there trembling with weakness and mute with awe. Unable to make a sound, I gazed after the strangely desolate figure of that seaman carrying an oar on his shoulder up a barren, rock-strewn ravine under the dreary leaden sky of Tremolino's last day. Thus, walking deliberately, with his back to the sea, Dominic vanished from my sight.

With the quality of our desires, thoughts, and wonder proportioned to our infinite littleness, we measure even time itself by our own stature. Imprisoned in the house of personal illusions, thirty centuries in mankind's history seem less to look back upon than thirty years of our own life. And Dominic Cervoni takes his place in my memory by the side of the legendary wanderer on the sea of marvels and terrors, by the side of the fatal and impious adventurer, to whom the evoked shade of the soothsayer predicted a journey inland with an oar on his shoulder, till he met men who had never set eyes on ships and oars. It seems to me I can see them side by side in the twilight of an arid land, the unfortunate possessors of the secret lore of the sea, bearing the emblem of their hard calling on their shoulders, surrounded by silent and curious men: even as I, too, having turned my back upon the sea, am bearing those few pages in the twilight, with the hope of finding in an inland valley the silent welcome of some patient listener.

Chapter XLVI

"*A* fellow has now no chance of promotion unless he jumps into the muzzle of a gun and crawls out of the touch-hole."

He who, a hundred years ago, more or less, pronounced the above words in the uneasiness of his heart, thirsting for professional distinction, was a young naval officer. Of his life, career, achievements, and end nothing is preserved for the edification of his young successors in the fleet of today — nothing but this phrase, which, sailorlike in the simplicity of personal sentiment and strength of graphic expression, embodies the spirit of the epoch. This obscure but vigorous testimony has its price, its significance, and its lesson. It comes to us from a worthy ancestor. We do not know whether he lived long enough for a chance of that promotion whose way was so arduous. He belongs to the great array of the unknown — who are great, indeed, by the sum total of the devoted effort put out, and the colossal scale of success attained by their insatiable and steadfast ambition. We do not know his name; we only know of him what is material for us to know — that he was never backward on occasions of desperate service. We have this on the authority of a distinguished seaman of Nelson's time. Departing this life as Admiral of the Fleet on the eve of the Crimean War, Sir Thomas Byam Martin has recorded for us amongst his all too short autobiographical notes these few characteristic words uttered by one young man of the many who must have felt that particular inconvenience of a heroic age.

The distinguished Admiral had lived through it himself, and was a good judge of what was expected in those days from men and ships. A brilliant frigate captain, a man of sound judgment, of dashing bravery and of serene mind, scrupulously concerned for the welfare and honor of the navy, he missed a larger fame only by the chances of the service. We may well quote on this day the words written of Nelson, in the decline of a well-spent life, by Sir T. B. Martin, who died just fifty years ago on the very anniversary of Trafalgar.

"Nelson's nobleness of mind was a prominent and beautiful part of his character. His foibles — faults if you like — will never be dwelt upon in any memorandum of mine," he declares, and goes on — "he whose splendid and matchless achievements will be remembered with admiration while there is gratitude in the hearts of Britons, or while a ship floats upon the ocean; he whose example on the breaking out of the war gave so chivalrous an impulse to the younger men of the service that all rushed into rivalry of daring which disdained every warning of prudence, and led to acts of heroic enterprise which tended greatly to exalt the glory of our nation."

These are his words, and they are true. The dashing young frigate captain, the man who in middle age was nothing loath to give chase single-handed in his seventy-four to a whole fleet, the man of enterprise and consummate judgment, the old Admiral of the Fleet, the good and trusted servant of his country under two kings and a queen, had felt correctly Nelson's influence, and expressed himself with precision out of the fullness of his seaman's heart.

"Exalted," he wrote, not "augmented." And therein his feeling and his pen captured the very truth. Other men there were ready and able to add to the treasure of victories the British navy has given to the nation. It was the lot of Lord Nelson to exalt all this glory. Exalt! the word seems to be created for the man.

Chapter XLVII

*T*he British navy may well have ceased to count its victories. It is rich beyond the wildest dreams of success and fame. It may well, rather, on a culminating day of its history, cast about for the memory of some reverses to appease the jealous fates which attend the prosperity and triumphs of a nation. It holds, indeed, the heaviest inheritance that has ever been entrusted to the courage and fidelity of armed men.

It is too great for mere pride. It should make the seamen of today humble in the secret of their hearts, and indomitable in their unspoken resolution. In all the records of history there has never been a time when a victorious fortune has been so faithful to men making war upon the sea. And it must be confessed that on their part they knew how to be faithful to their victorious fortune. They were exalted. They were always watching for her smile; night or day, fair weather or foul, they waited for her slightest sign with the offering of their stout hearts in their hands. And for the inspiration of this high constancy they were indebted to Lord Nelson alone. Whatever earthly affection he abandoned or grasped, the great Admiral was always, before all, beyond all, a lover of Fame. He loved her jealously, with an inextinguishable ardor and an insatiable desire — he loved her with a masterful devotion and an infinite trustfulness. In the plenitude of his passion he was an exacting lover. And she never betrayed the greatness of his trust! She attended him to the end of his life, and he died pressing her last gift (nineteen prizes) to his heart. "Anchor, Hardy — anchor!" was as much the cry of an ardent lover as of a consummate seaman. Thus he would hug to his breast the last gift of Fame.

It was this ardor which made him great. He was a flaming example to the wooers of glorious fortune. There have been great officers before — Lord Hood, for instance, whom he himself regarded as the greatest sea officer England ever had. A long succession of great commanders opened the sea to the vast range of Nelson's genius. His time had come; and, after the great sea officers, the great naval tradition passed into the keeping of a great man. Not the least glory of the navy is that it understood Nelson. Lord Hood trusted him. Admiral Keith told him: "We can't spare you either as Captain or Admiral." Earl St. Vincent put into his hands, untrammeled by orders, a division of his fleet, and Sir Hyde Parker gave him two more ships at Copenhagen than he had asked for. So much for the chiefs; the rest of the navy surrendered to him their devoted affection, trust, and admiration. In return he gave them no less than his own exalted soul. He breathed into them his own ardor and his own ambition. In a few short years he revolutionized, not the strategy or tactics of sea-warfare, but the very conception of victory itself. And this is genius. In that alone, through the fidelity of his fortune and the power of his inspiration, he stands unique amongst the leaders of fleets and sailors. He brought heroism into the line of duty. Verily he is a terrible ancestor.

And the men of his day loved him. They loved him not only as victorious armies have loved great commanders; they loved him with a more intimate feeling as one of themselves. In the words of a contemporary, he had "a most happy way of gaining the affectionate respect of all who had the felicity to serve under his command."

To be so great and to remain so accessible to the affection of one's fellow-men is the mark of exceptional humanity. Lord Nelson's greatness was very human. It had a moral basis; it needed to feel itself surrounded by the warm devotion of a band of brothers. He was vain and tender. The love and admiration which the navy gave him so unreservedly soothed the restlessness of his professional pride. He trusted them as much as they trusted him. He was a seaman of seamen. Sir T. B. Martin states that he never conversed with any officer who had served under Nelson "without hearing the heartiest expressions of attachment to his person and admiration of his frank and conciliatory manner to his subordinates." And Sir Robert Stopford, who commanded one of the ships with which Nelson chased to the West Indies a fleet nearly double in number, says in a letter: "We are half-starved and otherwise inconvenienced by being so long out of port, but our reward is that we are with Nelson."

This heroic spirit of daring and endurance, in which all public and private differences were sunk throughout the whole fleet, is Lord Nelson's great legacy, triply sealed by the victorious impress of the Nile, Copenhagen, and Trafalgar. This is a legacy whose value the changes of time cannot affect. The men and the ships he knew how to lead lovingly to the work of courage and the reward of glory have passed away, but Nelson's uplifting touch remains in the standard of achievement he has set for all time. The principles of strategy may be immutable. It is certain they have been, and shall be again, disregarded from timidity, from blindness, through infirmity of purpose. The tactics of great captains on land and sea can be infinitely discussed. The first object of tactics is to close with the adversary on terms of the greatest possible advantage; yet no hard-and-fast rules can be drawn from experience, for this capital reason, amongst others — that the quality of the adversary is a variable element in the problem. The tactics of Lord Nelson have been amply discussed, with much pride and some profit. And yet, truly, they are already of but archaic interest. A very few years more and the hazardous difficulties of handling a fleet under canvas shall have passed beyond the conception of seamen who hold in trust for their country Lord Nelson's legacy of heroic spirit. The change in the character of the ships is too great and too radical. It is good and proper to study the acts of great men with thoughtful reverence, but already the precise intention of Lord Nelson's famous memorandum seems to lie under that veil which Time throws over the clearest conceptions of every great art. It must not be forgotten that this was the first time when Nelson, commanding in chief, had his opponents under way — the first time and the last. Had he lived, had there been other fleets left to oppose him, we would, perhaps, have learned something more of his greatness as a sea officer. Nothing could have been added to his greatness as a leader. All that can be affirmed is, that on no other day of his short and glorious career was Lord Nelson more splendidly true to his genius and to his country's fortune.

Chapter XLVIII

*A*nd yet the fact remains that, had the wind failed and the fleet lost steerage way, or, worse still, had it been taken aback from the eastward, with its leaders within short range of the enemy's guns, nothing, it seems, could have saved the headmost ships from capture or destruction. No skill of a great sea officer would have availed in such a contingency. Lord Nelson was more than that, and his genius would have remained undiminished by defeat. But obviously tactics, which are so much at the mercy of irremediable accident, must seem to a modern seaman a poor matter of study. The Commander-in-Chief in the great fleet action that will take its place next to the Battle of Trafalgar in the history of the British navy will have no such anxiety, and will feel the weight of no such dependence. For a hundred years now no British fleet has engaged the enemy in line of battle. A hundred years is a long time, but the difference of modern conditions is enormous. The gulf is great. Had the last great fight of the English navy been that of the First of June, for instance, had there been no Nelson's victories, it would have been well-nigh impassable. The great Admiral's slight and passion-worn figure stands at the parting of the ways. He had the audacity of genius, and a prophetic inspiration.

The modern naval man must feel that the time has come for the tactical practice of the great sea officers of the past to be laid by in the temple of august memories. The fleet tactics of the sailing days have been governed by two points: the deadly nature of a raking fire, and the dread, natural to a commander dependent upon the winds, to find at some crucial moment part of his fleet thrown hopelessly to leeward. These two points were of the very essence of sailing tactics, and these two points have been eliminated from the modern tactical problem by the changes of propulsion and armament. Lord Nelson was the first to disregard them with conviction and audacity sustained by an unbounded trust in the men he led. This conviction, this audacity and this trust stand out from amongst the lines of the celebrated memorandum, which is but a declaration of his faith in a crushing superiority of fire as the only means of victory and the only aim of sound tactics. Under the difficulties of the then existing conditions he strove for that, and for that alone, putting his faith into practice against every risk. And in that exclusive faith Lord Nelson appears to us as the first of the moderns.

Against every risk, I have said; and the men of today, born and bred to the use of steam, can hardly realize how much of that risk was in the weather. Except at the Nile, where the conditions were ideal for engaging a fleet moored in shallow water, Lord Nelson was not lucky in his weather. Practically it was nothing but a quite unusual failure of the wind which cost him his arm during the Teneriffe expedition. On Trafalgar Day the weather was not so much unfavorable as extremely dangerous.

It was one of these covered days of fitful sunshine, of light, unsteady winds, with a swell from the westward, and hazy in general, but with the land about the Cape at times distinctly visible. It has been my lot to look with reverence upon the very spot more than once, and for many hours together. All but thirty years ago, certain exceptional circumstances made me very familiar for a time with that bight in the Spanish coast which would be enclosed within a straight line drawn from Faro to Spartel. My well-remembered experience has convinced me that, in that corner of the ocean, once the wind has got to the northward of west (as it did on the 20th, taking the British fleet aback), appearances of westerly weather go for nothing, and that it is infinitely more likely to veer right round to the east than to shift back again. It was in those conditions that, at seven on the morning of the 21st, the signal for the fleet to bear up and steer east was made. Holding a clear recollection of these languid easterly sighs rippling unexpectedly against the run of the smooth swell, with no other warning than a ten-minutes' calm and a queer darkening of the coast-line, I cannot think, without a gasp of professional awe, of that fateful moment. Perhaps personal experience, at a time of life when responsibility had a special freshness and importance, has induced me to exaggerate to myself the danger of the weather. The great Admiral and good seaman could read aright the signs of sea and sky, as his order to prepare to anchor at the end of the day sufficiently proves; but, all the same, the mere idea of these baffling easterly airs, coming on at any time within half an hour or so, after the firing of the first shot, is enough to take one's breath away, with the image of the rearmost ships of both divisions falling off, unmanageable, broadside on to the westerly swell, and of two British Admirals in desperate jeopardy. To this day I cannot free myself from the impression that, for some forty minutes, the fate of the great battle hung upon a breath of wind such as I have felt stealing from behind, as it were, upon my cheek while engaged in looking to the westward for the signs of the true weather.

Never more shall British seamen going into action have to trust the success of their valor to a breath of wind. The God of gales and battles favoring her arms to the last, has let the sun of England's sailing-fleet and of its greatest master set in unclouded glory. And now the old ships and their men are gone; the new ships and the new men, many of them bearing the old, auspicious names, have taken up their watch on the stern and impartial sea, which offers no opportunities but to those who know how to grasp them with a ready hand and an undaunted heart.

Chapter XLIX

*T*his the navy of the Twenty Years' War knew well how to do, and never better than when Lord Nelson had breathed into its soul his own passion of honor and fame. It was a fortunate navy. Its victories were no mere smashing of helpless ships and massacres of cowed men. It was spared that cruel favor, for which no brave heart had ever prayed. It was fortunate in its adversaries. I say adversaries, for on recalling such proud memories we should avoid the word "enemies," whose hostile sound perpetuates the antagonisms and strife of nations, so irremediable perhaps, so fateful — and also so vain. War is one of the gifts of life; but, alas! no war appears so very necessary when time has laid its soothing hand upon the passionate misunderstandings and the passionate desires of great peoples. "Le temps," as a distinguished Frenchman has said, "est un galant homme." He fosters the spirit of concord and justice, in whose work there is as much glory to be reaped as in the deeds of arms.

One of them disorganized by revolutionary changes, the other rusted in the neglect of a decayed monarchy, the two fleets opposed to us entered the contest with odds against them from the first. By the merit of our daring and our faithfulness, and the genius of a great leader, we have in the course of the war augmented our advantage and kept it to the last. But in the exulting illusion of irresistible might a long series of military successes brings to a nation the less obvious aspect of such a fortune may perchance be lost to view. The old navy in its last days earned a fame that no belittling malevolence dare cavil at. And this supreme favor they owe to their adversaries alone.

Deprived by an ill-starred fortune of that self-confidence which strengthens the hands of an armed host, impaired in skill but not in courage, it may safely be said that our adversaries managed yet to make a better fight of it in 1797 than they did in 1793. Later still, the resistance offered at the Nile was all, and more than all, that could be demanded from seamen, who, unless blind or without understanding, must have seen their doom sealed from the moment that the Goliath, bearing up under the bows of the Guerrier, took up an inshore berth. The combined fleets of 1805, just come out of port, and attended by nothing but the disturbing memories of reverses, presented to our approach a determined front, on which Captain Blackwood, in a knightly spirit, congratulated his Admiral. By the exertions of their valor our adversaries have but added a greater luster to our arms. No friend could have done more, for even in war, which severs for a time all the sentiments of human fellowship, this subtle bond of association remains between brave men — that the final testimony to the value of victory must be received at the hands of the vanquished.

Those who from the heat of that battle sank together to their repose in the cool depths of the ocean would not understand the watchwords of our day, would gaze with amazed eyes at the engines of our strife. All passes, all changes: the animosity of peoples, the handling of fleets, the forms of ships; and even the sea itself seems to wear a different and diminished aspect from the sea of Lord Nelson's day. In this ceaseless rush of shadows and shades, that, like the fantastic forms of clouds cast darkly upon the waters on a windy day, fly past us to fall headlong below the hard edge of an implacable horizon, we must turn to the national spirit, which, superior in its force and continuity to good and evil fortune, can alone give us the feeling of an enduring existence and of an invincible power against the fates.

Like a subtle and mysterious elixir poured into the perishable clay of successive generations, it grows in truth, splendor, and potency with the march of ages. In its incorruptible flow all round the globe of the earth it preserves from the decay and forgetfulness of death the greatness of our great men, and amongst them the passionate and gentle greatness of Nelson, the nature of whose genius was, on the faith of a brave seaman and distinguished Admiral, such as to "Exalt the glory of our nation."

CPSIA information can be obtained
at www.ICGtesting.com
Printed in the USA
BVHW081137270620
582374BV00002B/183